TOOTH AND NAIL

JESSICA RANEY

THIRD WHEEL PUBLISHING

For my Nan

CHAPTER 1

"SON OF A BITCH." Del banged her fists against the soggy ground. By the feel of the cool mud, sticks and thick grass blades against her stomach, she surmised she was naked. The mud smelled like garbage and fish, and she heard the gurgle of water, so she knew that she was on the riverbank. She flexed her legs just slightly and her muscles screamed in pain. Del pressed her forehead into the mud, clenched her fists, and flexed again. She knew she would be sore for days, but it would fade, and it would get better faster if she made an effort.

Del let the stretch go and exhaled. Her throat burned and her head pounded. She raised her head and the vertebrae in her neck popped back into their normal place. The pain in her back muscles almost made her stop, but she screamed, and that was all she was going to give it. When she got to her feet, she wobbled a bit, stabilized herself, and sucked in a big lungful of air. She smelled blood.

She looked down at herself. Her naked torso was covered in thick, clotted blood, as were her hands. She didn't need a mirror to know that her face, the lower half anyway, was covered in it too. She stumbled over to the edge of the water and her knees buckled. She cupped her hands and scooped some water. They were shaking, and she lost most of the water. She tried it two more times then cursed before she lowered her head to the water and slurped up a mouthful. The water mixed with the blood in her mouth and she spat it out a few times until the coppery taste was gone. The first swallow felt like sandpaper and burned on the way down her throat, but after a few more, it felt and tasted much better. Del drank greedily even though the water was turbid, luke-warm and had a fishy smell. Her thirst managed, she slid into the water and washed off the dried, clotted blood. She hissed at the pain, but the water and the motion made her feel better. When she waded out of the water, she shook herself and slicked her hair back with her palms.

Del sniffed the air. Based on the curve of the river and smell of cow shit in the air, she knew she was close to the Biehl farm. The naked walk out was going to be a mile or so. She would have to get something to wear, maybe at the Biehl's' place because she didn't think she had a clothing cache any closer than the farm. She picked her way along the river bank until she got to the barbed-wire fence that marked the boundary of Old Man Biehl's property. It was a tangled mess with the fence posts ripped completely out of the ground. The dirt was churned up and all the grass was trampled. Del bent down to look at the ground and saw no hoof prints that would indicate Biehl's cattle had done the damage. Instead, she saw the thing she knew she would see, a large print that looked like a human foot and a dog's foot and neither all at the same time.

"Fuck," she said.

She grabbed a fence post and shoved it back in its hole. She did the same with the other one and pushed the ground in around each. The barbed wire she couldn't do much with, Biehl would have to fix that on his own. She grabbed up big handfuls of dirt and erased the tracks in the ground. She followed the signs of flattened grass back through the field, and when she came to the clearing, she lowered her head and sighed.

The front half of the cow was at least three feet from the back half of the animal, and it had been gouged and ripped apart. The neck was intact and the area around the chest cavity had been torn, with big hunks of hide and flesh missing. Its belly had been ripped open and the intestines yanked out and strewn all over the field. The entire site had the look of a kill by an animal that hadn't been hungry, but rather delighted in the destruction. She shook her head sadly and walked on. There wasn't anything she could do to clean it up, and Biehl would miss the cow if she tried to dump it in the river. It was best to let it be. The old farmer would assume coyotes got it. They were thick all around.

Del continued through the field, and when she got to the outer buildings and barns, she slunk around in the early morning shadows until she got close to the house. Old Biehl was gone. She heard him puttering around in the outer barn. Only Viola, his wife, was in the house. Del opened the screen door slowly to avoid any squeaking, then cocked her ear and listened carefully. She could hear the old gal somewhere on the second floor, so she eased inside the kitchen and looked around. There were some pegs behind the door, but they were empty. A hallway led further into the house and she saw a closed door on the opposite side of the room from the hall. She crossed the kitchen and opened the door. It led to the basement. She didn't want to be trapped in a basement, but she figured that was where the washer and dryer was, so she decided to chance it. With any luck, she'd find something to cover herself, and there would be an outside door to escape through.

The old wooden steps creaked and shuddered under her weight. She winced and stopped halfway because they were so noisy. She listened carefully but couldn't hear anything. She really didn't have much choice but to keep going, so she tried to put as little weight as possible on the old wooden steps and descended as quickly as she could. She was in luck; there was a washer and dryer in the basement. She opened the dryer and found it empty, but when she opened the washer, she found sodden sheets. She looked around, found nothing else usable, cursed under her breath, then yanked a wet white sheet out of the washer. She managed to rip a hole in the sheet big enough for her head, then donned the makeshift dress. She searched around the musty old basement for a few more minutes and found some rope which she used as a belt, then her ensemble was complete. She knew she looked ridiculous, but ugly was less likely to get her arrested than naked, and she had a five mile walk back to the trailer park.

Her luck with the sheet dress was the end of her streak. She heard heavy footsteps above, then the basement light came on. She retreated behind the steps and waited as Viola heaved herself down the old stairs toward the washer. Del had left the washer lid up. The old lady paused and looked at it, obviously confused, then started looking around the basement. Del stood perfectly still. She didn't want to hurt the old woman, but she really didn't know how she was going to explain wearing a sheet in the old girl's basement. She'd likely kill the old woman if she whacked her in the head, but figured maybe if she just shoved her down, it wouldn't hurt too bad, then she could be up the steps and gone before anyone caught her.

Viola's back was to her and Del knew it was her only shot. She shoved the old lady down into a big pile of cardboard boxes. Viola yelled and floundered around. Del took off up the steps, taking them two at a time. She slammed the basement door behind her, then turned and ran out of the house as fast as she could. She rounded the house and met Old Man Biehl on his way back from the garage. She was moving too fast for him to even register what she was. She lowered her shoulder and slammed into him like an NFL linebacker. He went flying, completely upended, and by the time he got up, Del was down the gravel driveway and out of sight.

She hoped neither one of the old fogies was seriously hurt. That was never her intention, but sometimes it just couldn't be helped. She ran a couple of miles before her screaming muscles and burning lungs forced her to stop. The wet sheet was sticking to her all wrong and rubbing against her skin uncomfortably. She stopped and adjusted it. When she looked up, she saw a filthy, old Ford Ranger truck pull up beside her. She scowled at the driver when he rolled down the window. He spit a big wad of chew out at her feet and grinned.

"Got out, did ya?"

"Looks like, don't it?"

"Yup. Jerry sent me to find you on account of the daylight." Bobby Ring could have been anywhere from seventeen to thirty. His long face had rat-like features and beady eyes. He had a sparse mustache, and long greasy brown hair tucked under a filthy old NASCAR hat. He spit at her again and she stared him down.

"Spit at me again and see how you like it," she said.

Another man, same age and build, shoved around the driver and grinned at her. "You ought not be so surly Del. We's the ones with the truck, and you ain't got no clothes." Billy Ring was Bobby's twin, and equally as unattractive and stupid as his brother.

Del rolled her eyes. She could walk back home, but these idiots could get her home much faster. She walked around the truck to the passenger side. Billy got out and motioned for her to get in and ride in the middle. Bobby smiled at her again, showing his nasty brown teeth. Del got a whiff of the interior of the truck, a mixture of cigarette smoke, unwashed body, and pig shit. She also smelled the sickly-sweet smell of rot and knew that someplace under the seat, the Rings had stashed some dead animal. Or worse.

"No way am I riding up there between you." Del shook her head and climbed in the bed of the truck.

"We're liable to get pulled over. You best ride up here. We don't bite," Bobby said through the open back window.

"Yes, you do," Del said. "You also fucking stink. Nobody is going to stop you, and we ain't far from the trailer."

Billy smelled himself and shrugged, then got back in the truck and slammed the door.

"You pay the ticket if they catch us," Bobby yelled as he slammed the window shut.

Del settled in against the wheel well amidst the garbage and animal bones as Bobby gassed the truck and spun gravel everywhere.

It had been a hell of a start to the day.

CHAPTER 2

THE TRUCK PULLED into the spot in front of her trailer and Bobby hit the brakes hard. Del slammed into the back of the truck. When she got her balance, she pounded on the window and cracked the glass. "Dumbass," she yelled as she climbed down out of the truck bed.

"Gosh darn it, Del. You broke it!" Billy yelled as he and Bobby got out.

Del flipped them off and headed up the two concrete steps and into the trailer. It was dark inside. No light from the morning sun was coming in thanks to the blackout curtains. The only light in the room was the TV, which was playing the Today Show. She heard a hiss when she opened the door and let the light in. She slammed the door and turned on the overhead light.

Her cousin Jerry was sitting on the couch in his underwear amidst a sea of empty soda cans, porno magazines, and empty blood bags.

"It's a fucking sty in here," Del yelled as she flipped on the lights.

"Del, jeez, you got out. Looks like the boys found you," Jerry stammered as he yanked his pants on.

"Yeah. Thanks for sending those dipshits. How the fuck did I get out, Jerry?"

"How do you think? You broke out."

Del rolled her eyes as she rummaged around in one of the cabinets. She found a bottle of Jack Daniels with a few shots still left in it. She downed it. The liquor dulled the ache in her bones and muscles without giving her any mental numbness. That was also a curse. "No shit. The question is how did that happen? You had to have screwed up my tonic."

Jerry looked at her and then down at his feet. "I-I didn't. I figured it would be ok."

"You used old shit, didn't you?" Jerry didn't answer her, and she threw the empty whiskey bottle in the trash. "You know better than to use old shit. It don't work as good."

"It wasn't that old. One month don't make no difference Del."

"Well, apparently it does." Del was suddenly annoyed by the darkness and dank smell in the room. She stomped over to the big bay window, the nicest feature of the trailer besides the garden tub and yanked the heavy black curtains back. Jerry hissed and recoiled as the light streamed into the living room. Del rolled her eyes. "Give me a break. The sun don't burn you like that."

Jerry pulled the old afghan off the couch and threw it over himself. Only his face peeked out. "You don't know. It burns!"

"Oh, yeah, it must hurt like a bitch. Did it hurt this bad the time you spent the whole day watching Misty Singer sunbathe in her panties? Musta not burned bad enough to stop you from beating off for three hours straight."

"That was... look Del," Jerry sputtered and tried to look indignant. If he had been capable of blushing, he would have been beet red.

Del looked at the clock on the stove. It was almost 9, and she had to be at work at 10. "You got two jobs today. One, you best mix up a fresh batch of tonic for me. Two, you need to go see what the shed looks like. It's gonna need fixed." She grabbed a jar of pickles out of the refrigerator and took a big swig of the juice. She grimaced at the sour taste but took another big swig. The pickle juice would help her torn and abused muscles recuperate.

"Now how am I supposed to go out in daylight and fix that shed?" Jerry put his hands on his hips and looked at Del like she had lost her mind.

Just then, Bobby and Billy came in the door. Bobby belched and Del nearly threw up at the smell of his burp and the general rotten, pig shit smell that accompanied Billy and Bobby wherever they went. Del finished off the rest of the pickle juice then pointed at the two boys. "Make them do it."

She looked at the boys. "What did I tell you two dipshits about coming inside my house?"

"Aww, come on Del," Jerry motioned toward the boys. "That ain't fair."

"They stink. They eat dead shit. They already ruined two chairs with their skank asses. You can visit with 'em outside, you want to jaw so bad." Del tossed the pickle jar in the trash and headed back to her room as Jerry protested loudly. She slammed her door closed and shrugged off her makeshift dress. She was filthy. Mud caked her legs and feet. That would all wash off. What wouldn't were the deep black bruises that covered her body. They were most prevalent around her sternum and chest, and she knew they were all over her spine as well. She stretched and nearly screamed as the bones and muscles let her know that they had been stressed to the maximum amount. The tonic should have helped her.

Fucking Jerry. Lazy was the right word for him. He had always been lazy. Her gran had told them both many times how fussy the tonic was. You had to pick the wolfsbane a month before and let it dry. The tonic had to be made as close to the cycle as possible, and it took a solid four hours to brew. Jerry knew all that, too. He also knew that the tonic wasn't something you could dump into a Tupperware and keep for later. Gran had drilled it into him every time she made it. He knew all of it, but he was also a deadbeat who hung out with disgusting ghouls, so where she might have once trusted Jerry, she now knew she couldn't. It presented a significant problem as she was planning her move. She needed a reliable source for the monthly tonic and she couldn't brew it herself. The one time she had tried, she suffered convulsions and fever for a week just from picking the wolfsbane.

She felt better after the hot shower but couldn't shake the thought that something worse had happened last night. If the only thing she killed was a cow, she would be lucky. There were two more nights in the cycle, and the worst was yet to come. She dressed quickly in her uniform and pulled her wet blonde hair up into a bun.

Her room was cramped. Not that there was a great deal of furniture—Del owned only a queen-size bed and an ancient old nightstand she inherited from her grandmother —but the room was littered with moving boxes. Some were packed and marked. Some were half packed, some were empty, and some were just folded up pieces of cardboard. She had three weeks until she moved and had barely made a dent in packing or preparations. She wasn't sure what was holding her back. Every morning when she woke up, she smiled at the calendar tacked on the wall and the day, her moving day, circled there. Only a few more weeks of ringing up cheap hamburger and cigarettes at the IGA. Only a few more weeks of dealing with her mama. Only a few more weeks of listening to Jerry play Xbox games and beat off to the Today Show. Only a few more weeks of navigating muddy dirt roads that never seemed to dry out, of listening to the shitty local radio station that was still playing the same music from five years ago as if it were brand-new, of going no place and doing nothing except working, coming home, and dreaming of progress. Del didn't exactly know what progress was, but somewhere in her mind, progress was tied to a city and a degree. She was determined to get to one and acquire the other. The city meant freedom and options. The degree, she thought, meant money, and money, she thought, meant security.

Her phone rang, and the number on the caller ID gave her a little flutter of hope in her guts and a slight smile. She shoved things in her bag as she answered.

"Hello? Oh, yes ma'am. How are you?... Uh, yes, I have the paperwork you sent. I just need to fax it back to you... today? ... well, umm... yes, no, no it's not a problem... sure thing... yes, I'll send a money order... yep, I mean, yes ma'am, today... ok, yes... thanks, you too... bye now."

She'd found a tiny garage apartment a few blocks from the school in Pittsburgh, and rented it sight unseen. It could be full of roaches and smell like cat piss for all Del cared. It was still better than here. She didn't have a job lined up yet, but she had a long, storied career in service and retail, so she was confident she would find something after she moved. The phone call made her happy, but when she got back out to the living room, she got business-like again.

Jerry was still wrapped in the afghan and the boys were standing near the door. They hadn't left the mat area. "Jerry. New tonic. Fix the shed. You ain't got nothing else to do til them two are done." She picked up her wallet and keys and tossed them in her bag.

"You know Del, you can't just boss me like this. I got limits as to what I can—" Jerry yelped when Del grabbed his head and smashed it against the floor.

She was breathing heavily, and it took every ounce of self-control that she possessed not to keep smashing Jerry's head in. "You got limits? Well so do I. And they got crossed this morning when I had to beat up a couple of old people because you was too lazy to brew fresh tea. Quit bitching and just do what you're supposed to for once."

She let Jerry up. The side of his head had a gash in it, but it healed within a quickly. He rubbed the place. "Dammit Del. You're too damn testy during the Moons."

"That's right. And it's worse cause you can't brew right." Del grabbed her bag and wrinkled her nose at the two ghouls. "You two, go fix the shed." She looked back over her shoulder at Jerry. "Can't happen again Jerry."

"I know it," Jerry said as she went out the door. "You don't gotta be so mean about it though."

Del got in her decrepit Chevy truck and started the engine. It gave a few coughs and sputters before she was able to coax it to life. "I do. But I sure wish I didn't have to be." She slammed the door and then roared off out of the trailer park, already ten minutes late for work.

CHAPTER 3

BY THE TIME Del finished her shift at the IGA, she had almost called Jerry and told him not to make her tonic or fix the shed. Every single person who crossed her path seemed to want her to snap and rip their trachea out of their throat. Only the fact that it was her last two weeks of work had kept her from punching Skippy Bowman in the mouth when he laid into her about being late. It wasn't that she wasn't late. She was, but she had made up a little time on her drive and was only about fifteen minutes late. And while she knew that late was late, and she was willing to put up with a little shit, she didn't think she deserved the constant barrage of verbal abuse Skippy heaped on her throughout her shift.

"You just think you can come in here any time you like, don't you Delilah?" He pursed his lips and tapped his pen on his clipboard.

"Look, Skippy, I said I was sorry for being late. You don't gotta bring it up every fifteen minutes," Del said as she scanned groceries and sacked them.

"Well, I guess I do, because you are habitually late." He poked his pen at her. "And what did I tell you about calling me Skippy?"

"Same thing I told you about calling me Delilah," she snapped. She squeezed her hand, and the can of corn she scanned dented in her hand. She tossed it into the bin at her feet and tried to smile at the customer. "Sorry ma'am. You don't want a dented can. Mr. Bowman, can you grab another can of DelMonte corn for this lady, please?"

Skippy's mouth was hanging open as he stared at the can of corn. He shuffled off to get the replacement can and kept his distance from Del the rest of the day, which was probably for the best. She only had two weeks left at the stupid job and then she'd never see fat, pimply Skippy Bowman again. The rest of the shift passed in relative calm. Customers tested her nerves, as always, which was certainly made worse by her place in the moon cycle, but she controlled her temper.

She got a text from Jerry that the tonic was ready and the shed fixed. She also got a voicemail from her mom claiming an emergency, but Del knew it wasn't. Still, she stopped by once her shift was over. Her mom sat in the ancient, stained recliner in her bedroom. The rest of the house was empty. Her mom only lived in the master bedroom. It was a cramped mess that contained a queen-sized bed, the disgusting smoke- infused Lazy Boy, a few rusted TV trays, and a gigantic 50-inch flat screen TV, the only piece added in the last ten years. Her mom was smoking, as always, the ashtray that had been around longer than Del had been alive overflowed with cigarette butts.

"So what's the emergency, Mom?" Del said as she automatically began to clean. She picked up the used Kleenex and Little Debbie wrappers that littered the floor around the trashcan and emptied and wiped out the ashtray.

"Well, I've had another heart attack," her mom said as she exhaled a long plume of smoke, then immediately took another drag so long that it finished the cigarette. She stubbed it out in the clean ashtray and lit another.

"Then you shoulda called 911 and not me," Del said. Her mom had a self-diagnosed heart attack every day.

"I could have died, Delilah," Peg huffed. "But what do you care? You're leaving anyways."

Del had been through this same conversation enough times to know that there was nothing she could say to not get mired in an argument. She didn't have time for it tonight, and her temper wouldn't take it anyway, so she said the only thing she could. "I'll check in on you tomorrow, Mom. Call Jerry if you need something."

"That lazy shit? He don't do nothing except smoke dope all day. Sits around."

Del almost laughed out loud that her mother couldn't see the irony of the insult, but she stopped herself. "Bye, Mom," she said as she left the room and closed the bedroom door behind her.

Del had time for one more stop at the gas station where she picked up some V8 juice and a jar of pickles. She had about an hour to change clothes and get to the shed. Her phone rang three times in five minutes, which meant it was Shelby. She rolled her eyes on the fifth call, picking it up as she pulled a ratty t-shirt over her head. "What?"

The rapid-fire barrage of insults that came streaming through the phone speaker made her roll her eyes again. Like with her mother, Del knew better than to engage.

"Not tonight... No... NO. I can't... just... Shelby, I ain't got time for this. I'll call you tomorrow." Del hung up the phone and turned it off. She wouldn't be able to answer anyway, and she knew Shelby would continue to blow up her phone all night.

The cramps started on the hike back through the woods behind the trailer. It was about a thirty-minute walk out to her shed. She stopped three times, doubled over in pain as a cramp hit her. She gripped a small tree and snapped it in half. She needed to hurry. The pains were only about three minutes apart when she finally made it to the shed. Her clothes were wet with sweat and she struggled as she pulled them off. She barely had time to lock at the door. It wasn't a shed so much as an old shipping container, brought up the mountain in pieces. The big door had come off its hinges from her pounding it last night before. The boys fixed it, or at least put it back on the hinges, but it would barely open.

She squeezed through and yanked the door shut. It shut, but she had a tough time getting the hasp and the padlocks closed. Her hands were shaking as she closed the fourth and final lock. She spun around, frantic to find the tonic. It was there, in the old dented thermos. She grabbed it and chugged it.

She wondered what the concoction tasted like if you weren't cursed. Maybe it tasted like herbal tea, floral or woodsy, but she would never know. To her and to anyone else it was brewed to subdue, the wolfsbane tonic tasted like a combination of vomit and cow shit. She gagged as the liquid burned its way into her stomach, and the cramps increased in frequency. She screamed and dropped to the metal floor. She pounded it and made a dent. As the tonic took effect, her ability to dent the floor lessened. Finally, there was just the pain as her bones shifted and muscles tore. She screamed and panted and screamed some more, but there was nobody around to hear her until finally, mercifully, she lost consciousness.

CHAPTER 4

THE FIRST THING Del noticed when she woke up was that she was laying on metal this time, not mud. That was good. She raised her head and saw the door was barely on the hinges; one hasp and padlock remained and that was all that was holding the door on. Morning light streamed through the opening and she could hear the birds chirping outside. She pushed herself up off the metal floor and got to her feet. Her clean clothes were stashed in the tool chest outside. She struggled to get the lock open as waves of pain and nausea hit her. The tonic had done its job, but just barely. She had been awfully close to busting out. Maybe Jerry had fucked up again with the tonic brew, but she doubted it. He was a lazy shit, sure, but he wasn't a total waste, and he had been her best friend for their entire lives. He knew what it would do to her if she hurt anyone ever again. If he messed up the brew, he didn't know it. She dressed and picked her way back home through the scrub brush and trees. Jerry was in the dark again, but the trailer was clean.

"Did it work?" he asked hesitantly as he handed her a glass of pickle juice.

She waved it off. She had thrown up three times on the hike back home. "Mostly. I still broke three locks."

He looked panicked. "I swear Del, I did it right. Just like Gran showed us."

She nodded. "I know. Something else is going on. Just gotta get through this last night."

"But what then? You gotta figure it out before you try to leave."

"I will. We'll go talk to Aunt Jewel. She'll maybe know something." It was seven in the morning and she didn't have to be at work until noon. "Wake me up at 10:30 if I ain't up." She took a quick shower to rinse off, then collapsed in the bed.

She woke up abruptly, not via alarm or Jerry, but by something pouncing on her back and slapping at her head.

In an instant, she turned her body over and grabbed the hands that were hitting her. The woman sitting on top of her was so angry she was beet red. She couldn't slap anymore with Del holding her wrists, but she could bounce and move her legs, so she started doing that. Del flipped and reversed their positions. "Goddamn it Shelby, what the hell is the matter with you?" she growled.

The small blonde underneath her squirmed and tried to

move, but Del had her pinned. "I called your dumb ass all night. Where the hell were you that you couldn't answer?"

Del rolled her eyes. She hadn't seen Shelby in two weeks. Her husband was home for his month break, so Shelby was playing the good wife. "You don't own me, Shelby. I don't answer to you."

"The fuck you don't. Who was you with Del? Was it that bitch from Athens that works at the Par Mar? I seen her eyeing you that last time we was in there."

The rules of the relationship were simple. Shelby was married to Derek, who made a ton of money working on coal barges that went up and down the river. He was gone a month at a time, and in that time, Shelby was all over Del. When Derek came home, Shelby dropped Del and made him feel at home. In that month, Del was expected to sit quietly and wait, and she was most definitely not allowed to be jealous. Shelby, however, could be as jealous as humanly possible, most of the time, without any just cause. Del had been trying to get rid of Shelby for a year, but Shelby was persistent. She was also ridiculously hot and great in bed.

"I wasn't with anybody," Del said, pressing Shelby's hands down into the mattress. "I was sleeping. Turned off the phone. Damnit, stop squirming. I don't feel good." All the movement made her muscles scream, and her stomach was still queasy.

Del must have looked convincingly ill, because Shelby stopped moving and eyed her cautiously. "You swear you was sick?"

"I swear," Del said. She let go of Shelby and laid back down. The room was spinning.

"Well why didn't you just say so, baby," Shelby cooed. Del felt a hand on her forehead and another one on her stomach. "I would have come over and taken care of you."

Del gave a little laugh. "You definitely ain't a nurse. Besides, ain't Derek in town?"

"He got called back out yesterday morning. He's going for the overtime." Shelby was rubbing slow circles on her stomach. "I missed you."

Del exhaled slowly as Shelby began to kiss her neck and she started to move her hand lower. Del grabbed her hand and stopped her. "Seriously, Shelby, I don't feel good."

"I bet I can make you feel better," Shelby said into her ear. Del was very tempted to let her try, but she was nauseated and sore. And she knew Shelby would ask too many questions about the horrible bruises that littered her body. She'd need a few days to heal before Shelby saw her naked. Shelby crawled on top of her and tried a few more ways to change Del's mind. Finally, Del sat up and grabbed Shelby's hands.

"Look, I just can't," Del said. The world was spinning again, and she swallowed down the urge to vomit as well as the urge to throw Shelby down and finish what had been started. "I ain't seen or heard from you in two weeks, and you come over here first wanting to beat on me, then wanting fuck me?"

Shelby's eyes narrowed. "You knew Derek was home. You

ain't seemed to mind this arrangement for the past three years."

"Yeah, well, times change," Del said. "Besides, I'm leaving in a few weeks. We already talked about this."

"You talked. I didn't agree to nothing," Shelby said. "You just think you can leave me here while you go off to the fancy college and fuck whoever you want? I don't think so, Delilah."

"Well, yeah, I fucking think so. You're married Shelby. Did you think I was just gonna go along with this shit forever?" Del got up and looked for her uniform. She needed to get to work anyway.

"No. You ain't going anywhere until I say so." Shelby jumped up and grabbed Del's shirt before Del could put it on.

"Give that back," Del said in an exasperated tone. When Shelby was like this, it never ended well.

"No. Not til you say you ain't going anywhere."

"I'm paid up until month end. Then I'm leaving," Del said. She gave up on the shirt and went to the closet for another one. She put it on, then Shelby jumped on her back and start slapping her again. "Jesus Christ! You fucking crazy bitch." She shook Shelby off, but the woman jumped at her again and scratched her face. Del snapped. She grabbed Shelby and pinned her to the wall, then drew back a hand without thinking. She stopped when she saw the triumph on Shelby's face. Shelby loved rough and tumble, and she wasn't the least bit afraid of Del. Del lowered her hand and then threw up all over Shelby's feet.

Shelby's triumph morphed into disgust. "Ugh, Del, what the fuck?"

"I told you I was sick. Just fucking go, okay? Please Shelby. Leave me alone." Del threw up again, thick, black vomit.

"Well don't think this conversation is over, because it ain't," Shelby said. She kicked off her vomit covered shoes and left them in Del's room as she walked into the bathroom to rinse off her feet. When she came out, she pointed at Del and kept her distance. "I'm going to be back tomorrow."

Shelby stomped out the door. Del cleaned up a bit then walked out into the living room. Jerry didn't look up from his video game. "I tried to stop her."

"Not very fucking hard," Del said as she walked out and went to work.

CHAPTER 5

DEL LEFT work and about a mile from home, her stomach clenched and she got a funny feeling. A strange wave of sickness hit her, and unlike the normal waves of nausea during the cycle, this one wasn't the panicked sick she normally felt. It was a butterflies-in-the stomach feeling, like going over a hill quickly. Trepidatious, a bit of dread, but still thrilling. That feeling went away when she pulled in the entrance of the trailer park and sniffed the air. It was replaced by cold anger.

Two trucks were parked in the drive and one in the limited yard of the trailer. The two in the driveway were caked with mud and had empty beer cans and trash littering their beds. The one parked in the middle of her yard was a huge black beast with jacked up tires and chrome running boards. It was immaculately clean. There was only one person who drove a vehicle like that around town, and Del wanted no part of a visit from him.

Del got out of her old truck and slammed the door. A deep growl formed in her throat and she bristled for a fight as she stalked up the steps to the trailer. When she opened the door, she stood in the doorway and surveyed the scene.

Jerry was tied to one of the kitchen chairs with zip ties that cut deeply into his skin. He was clad in only his tighty-whitey underwear. Blood dripped down his face, and there was blood all over his pasty white body. The wounds that caused the blood had healed over, but Del growled aloud as one of the men, an asshole in a backward baseball cap, slashed across Jerry's chest with a huge Bowie knife, opening a deep wound that gushed blood.

There were four of them. She didn't know the backward cap asshole's name, but she knew the others. Donnie Antill, Mickey Jenkins, and Fat Eddie Warner were standing in her living room, torturing her cousin. They were all laughing and having a great time, but when she walked in, they all sniffed the air, turned, and growled at her. She snarled back, and they started to advance.

"Now, let's not do nothing idiotic here, boys," a voice said smoothly. Del turned and regarded the speaker. The voice belonged to Junior Nolan, who was sitting on her sofa, his legs crossed casually as he thumbed through one of Jerry's porno magazines. He was dressed all in black: black tank, black jeans, and highly polished black cowboy boots with a sharp, shiny silver toe.

"Imagine how Delilah here must feel, coming home to unexpected company."

"Company is welcome. You ain't," Del said. "What business do you got with him?"

"Always getting right to the point." Junior grinned and pointed at her with the rolled up porno mag. "I like that Delilah. You always was direct." He pointed at Jerry. "Your cousin, the bloodsucker here, went into business with me. Didn't hold up his end of the agreement."

Del's heart sank. There was only one joint venture to which Junior could be referring. She looked over at Jerry. "Tell me you ain't stupid enough to have done it."

Jerry looked down at his feet and said nothing.

"Oh, he's stupid enough," Junior said. "He's also stupid enough not to have the money he owes me."

"How much?" Del asked.

"Well, I calculate it to be about fifteen grand." He waved the magazine around the room. "Now he ain't spent it on nothing around this shithole. So, I'd really like to know, where is my money?"

Del walked over to the pack and bared her teeth at them. They growled back but parted so she had access to Jerry. "Where the fuck is it Jerry?"

"It ain't... I don't got it."

"Yeah, no fucking shit, dumbass. If you ain't got his money, you better have the crank. Where is it?"

"I ain't got that either. I sent... I sent the boys with it to Charleston. They only come back with a grand or so."

"Goddammit Jerry."

"It ain't my fault, Del! It ain't. I thought I could unload it easy at the store, but Buster found out."

Del rolled her eyes and turned back around to Junior. "Look, he ain't got it. I got about two. Take it and go find the Ring brothers. They got the rest."

"That ain't the way this works, Delilah. See, Jerry here made a Gentlemen's Agreement. He's gonna pay what he owes and if he don't, then we are gonna see how long it really takes to fry his pasty ass. It'll be worth my money to see that." He got up and walked over to them. He smiled down at her, then growled low through the smile, daring her to move.

Del stood her ground and growled right back, but without the smile.

He laughed. "Now come on. We don't need to do it like this. Be a real waste. Dad wouldn't like it."

"I don't give a fuck what he would like. Take the money and get out. I'll get you the rest," she said.

He kept smiling at her and nodded. "Yeah. Yeah, you sure will. You're both coming with us."

The rest of the pack moved in. Del dug in and braced herself for the fight she knew was coming.

"Don't try it Delilah. There's five of us. You know how that's gonna go if you put up a fuss," he said.

"I know how it's gonna go either way," she said as her eyes darted around the room at the four men closing in.

"Could be you don't know as much as you think you know. It could go good, too. All up to you."

Del didn't want to admit it, but he was right. There was a zero percent chance that she could deal with all of them, and it would just end badly for her and Jerry. It might still end badly, but she knew that the smart play was to wait and see. She relaxed a bit, relaxed her fists, and backed up. "Fine, but make it quick. I got shit to do."

CHAPTER 6

DEL SQUEEZED in the middle of one truck. They threw a comforter over Jerry and tossed him in the other truck. She knew where they were going, and she knew that despite this being the smart choice, none of the preceding choices she made, or Jerry had made, were smart at all. If by some miracle the situation worked out and both made it out alive, she was fairly sure she was going to kill Jerry.

He had been pretty good at coming up with idiotic schemes in the past. He tried to buy junk at flea markets and turn it around on eBay. He tried to fleece old ladies out of their welfare checks by claiming to be able to talk to the dead. Even his turn had been a stupid choice. Jerry worked at the Lion's Den porn store in Macksburg before he became a vampire. He always said he did it ironically, but Del was sure he didn't really know what that word meant, and she was even more sure that Jerry was just one of those people in the world that actually did like working in a porn store and had zero ambition to transcend his situation. He was impulsive, and even though she loved him, he was fucking dumb. He never thought through anything, which had been fine for a while, when his biggest problem was not spending all the rent money on video games and porn, but was something else entirely when the problem at hand was becoming a vampire.

Jerry believed a trucker from Pittsburgh who told him he could turn him. The trucker came in twice a week for German gay porn DVDs. The guy was sloppy fat with an acne scarred face, so she wasn't sure why Jerry believed that he had anything great to look forward to as a vampire. Jerry was blubbery and pasty and had curly red hair. If he thought getting turned was going to change any of that, he had been sorely mistaken. The trucker promised to turn him if Jerry let him fuck him, and Jerry did. The thing was, Jerry wasn't even gay, but he figured sucking a cock was a small price to pay for immortality.

The trucker kept his word, and after what Jerry described as the worst thirty minutes of his life in the porn store shitter, the trucker turned him. The problem was, nothing much changed, or at least, not the way Jerry had planned. He stayed fat and got even pastier. He couldn't die, and he healed fast, but he burned very slowly in the sun and got disgusting cold sores. He didn't gain any super powers like mind control or flight or anything else cool. He was stronger, but still not as strong as Del, although he could see better in the dark.

The trucks pulled off the main road and headed up the mountain on a gravel road that was surprisingly well maintained for the area. Del figured since Junior drove it regularly, he wouldn't abide a messed-up front end, like everybody else in the county dealt with. She was surprised he hadn't made them pave it over to save his precious black monstrosity the mud splatters, but paving reeked of money, and Galen liked a low profile.

The road wound around a bit, up and down the hillside, but they finally made it to the place she never ever wanted to end up. It was a little valley, a cleared-out hollow littered with doublewides, travel trailers, and rusty sheds. The trucks had to dodge several dogs, guinea fowl, and chickens before stopping in front of the least dilapidated dwelling.

Galen Nolan sat at a worn-out picnic table, skinning squirrels with an ancient pen knife. The squirrels disappeared in his gigantic square hands, and he removed the skin in under a minute. He had a whole bucket of dead squirrels and a cigarette dangled from the corner of his mouth as he flicked his knife, broke the tail, and pulled the pelt off in one motion. When he finished, he tossed the skins in a pile and the carcass in a bucket. He didn't look up when Junior led them over, he just kept skinning and smoking.

"Daddy, we got a problem," Junior said.

"Seems like you do," Galen said. The cigarette ash

dropped onto a squirrel. He brushed it aside and continued skinning it. "Delilah. How's your mother?"

"Same as she was when you left her," Del replied.

Galen barely shrugged in response. Junior brushed off the seat of the picnic table and sat down. "Delilah here owes us."

"No, Jerry does," she said.

"Well, now, you already said you would assume his debt. Course, if you ain't gonna do that, we can just fry him and be done with it." He motioned toward one of the boys holding Jerry to take off the blanket. Jerry thrashed and squawked.

"Hurt him and see what you get," Del growled and started toward Junior.

"Shut the fuck up, all of you," Galen said. He slammed a dead squirrel down on the table and pointed at the boys with his knife. "Put the bloodsucker in the shed." He looked at Del and Junior. "I don't forgive debts, not even by family."

"I got two grand. Take it and leave us the fuck alone."

"You owe fifteen, Delilah. How you think two is gonna be enough?" Junior laughed.

"Look, either it is or it ain't, and if it ain't, I can't change it. Take it or kill us. I'm already tired of dealing with you."

"Oh, it would be my pleasure," Junior stood up and pulled a gun out of his waistband. He pointed it at Del's head and grinned.

"Put that down you idiot. You ain't shooting her. Not yet." He pointed to Del. "The bloodsucker ain't going to pay. I keep him, and he cooks for us."

Del knew Jerry was too dumb to cook. He could barely make her tonic. He'd blow himself sky high if they put him to cooking; wouldn't last the week. Galen knew it too. He was betting on the choice she was about to make, and while she hated that she was going to make it, she didn't see another option. Her face reddened with rage and she said nothing, but they both knew what she was going to do. He said it for her.

"You can earn back the money."

"How?"

"Same way your brother does." Galen nodded toward Junior.

"No," she said, shaking her head. "I won't. I'm moving. I ain't staying here."

Galen shrugged. "You're going to have to wait til I get my money back. You was always smart for a girl. Shouldn't take you that long to get it back." He lit another cigarette and went back to skinning his squirrels. "Or say no and I burn the fat bloodsucker now."

He meant it. She saw him burn a cat once. An old stray tom she befriended. He threw it into a bonfire and laughed. When it crawled out, barely alive, he wouldn't let her put it out of its misery. He made her watch it until it died. It took all night. She knew he'd do the same to Jerry.

"When I bring you back your money, that's it. I'm done. Come near me again and I'll kill you," Del said. She looked him squarely in the eye. Her gaze never wavered.

He smiled and stared back. "I believe you'd try Delilah." He nodded at Junior. "Take her out back."

The four boys rushed her. She fought them. Kicked, bit, hit one in the nuts so hard he puked, but together they were too strong. They dragged her out behind one of the sheds, past a bunch of hunting dogs, chained up and mean. They snapped and snarled at them as they passed through their realm, pulling and straining at the chains. One came close to Junior and he hit it solidly in the side with a pipe. It yelped and snapped at him again, but retreated.

They held her while Junior beat her with the pipe. He gave her a good whack to her stomach, and when she doubled over, he hit her on back. She felt her ribs crack and when he hit her kidneys, she screamed and dropped to her knees. They grabbed one of her arms and held it out. He swung hard at her arm and connected right below her elbow. She screamed again as she felt the bones in her arm break. He didn't use the pipe on her face. He used his fists for that, smashing her nose and cheeks. When she collapsed into the dirt they took turns kicking her, laughing as they did, turning her body into a bloody, swollen mass of pain. When they were finished, she lay sputtering, coughing, and sucking short, pained breaths.

Junior grabbed a handful of her hair and yanked her head up. He nodded. "I reckon that's a good start."

She looked up at him, only able to see through one eye. Everything was foggy and far away feeling, but her hatred of him was what she clung to as she fought to remain conscious. She sucked in the biggest breath she could muster, then spit blood all over him, covering his face and shirt. She laughed and wheezed as he cursed. He drew back his fist and hit her squarely in the temple. After that, everything went black.

CHAPTER 7

DEL HAD no idea how long she'd been laying in the dirt. She faded in and out of consciousness and could barely make out blurry images with her one good eye. She felt hands grab her and pull her up. The motion was so painful, she screamed. They dragged her across the rocky mountain soil. Every bounce and snag was agony and she screamed the whole way. When they stopped, she heard a woman's voice.

"What's he want done?" the woman asked.

"Said you'd know."

An exasperated, sad sigh. "Bring her in then. Put her on the bed in the back."

Del mumbled and moaned as they hauled her up a few steps. The rest of the trip was short, and they unceremoniously tossed her onto a bed. She wheezed and tried to get a breath, but she couldn't, and it scared her. She jumped when she felt a cool hand on her forehead.

"Don't panic. Breathe slowly. You'll be all right," the woman said calmly. "You didn't have to throw her around like that."

"No, but we wanted to," one of them said. Del couldn't make out which one. She decided it didn't matter. They would all get what was coming to them, especially Junior. She used it, that rage. It helped her manage the pain.

"You two can leave."

"Junior said you better fix her up."

"Tell Galen I know my business."

Del heard them stomp back down the hallway, then the waves of pain and her throbbing body made her unable to sense much of anything. She cried and jumped in surprise and fear when she felt a weight on the bed next to her. Strong arms lifted her and cradled her throbbing head. Even though the movement was gentle, it pulled at her devastated ribs and back. She coughed and cried.

"It'll be okay. Drink this for me."

Del felt a cup touch her lips. She could barely smell through her ruined nose, but the liquid smelled earthy and sort of like mildew. She made a feeble attempt to push it away. "No. Just leave me alone."

"I know it doesn't smell nice. It doesn't taste nice either, but it will help you. I promise it will."

Del opened her eye and tried to see who was talking. The woman was just a dark shape. Despite that, she seemed calm and her voice was kind. If they had meant to kill her, Junior would have done it. He meant for her to suffer. Maybe this woman was another person to bring about more of that, but Del's instinct told her that wasn't the case.

"Look, it'll knock you out. Makes the pain go away for a bit. Come on now. Please?"

Another cough and Del screamed again at the pain from the movement. Death was better than this. Del nodded and pressed her lips to the cup. It was almost as bad as her tonics. It tasted like stagnant dish water—soapy, stale, and dank—but she drank it all.

When she finished, the woman eased her down onto the pillows. Del felt a cool, wet cloth on her face and forehead, and she calmed. It didn't take long for the stuff to do its job. As she got a numb, heavy feeling, she listened as the woman hummed an old mountain tune that Del remembered her Gran singing and she let it calm her as the medicine put her to sleep.

CHAPTER 8

WHEN SHE WOKE UP, it was daylight. Late afternoon, because the light was soft and muted and slightly orange. Whether it was the same afternoon or a different one, she had no idea because she had slept as soundly as she had ever slept in her life. Her arm was in a cast and throbbed with pain, but it was manageable. She was able to see again—both eyes would open—but when she tried to sit up, the pain was enough to make her cry out, so she lay still and tried to have a look around.

She knew she was in a trailer. The room was narrow, small, and lined with the same cheap paneling she had in her own place. The window was half-sized and had a hand crank, and there was a small bathroom off to the side. The difference was that everything was bright and clean instead of dark and cluttered. The bedsheets were crisp and white, yet soft, and the bed itself was a roomy queen size and comfortable. It took up most of the space in the room, but because everything looked so white and clean, the room seemed bigger. The room smelled clean and fresh too, with an herbaceous, pleasantly earthy smell.

As someone who was used to waking up naked and unable to remember exactly what happened, Del wasn't particularly shocked to be waking up in a strange bed, but she was surprised to be waking up with different clothes on. She wore a clean white t-shirt and a pair of blue running shorts, which were baggy on her. There was music coming from the other room, soft, classical music, not what she expected, and she could hear the clink of glass against glass and the sound of water running as someone did dishes.

Del made another attempt at getting up, and did manage to half-way sit up, but the pain was so intense she couldn't catch her breath and the world started to spin. She grabbed at the little bedside table to keep from falling but missed and knocked over the lamp, which crashed to the floor as she collapsed back against the pillows. The water shut off and light footsteps pattered down the hall. A woman leaned on the door frame and crossed her arms. The woman was tall, with medium length, chestnut brown hair pulled back into a low ponytail. A long, jagged scar ran down the right side of her face from her cheekbone to her chin. The other side of her face was smooth and unmarked. She stared at Del disapprovingly, but with a slightly amused smirk.

"It's not a good idea for you to get up yet," she said. Her

accent sounded funny to Del. She didn't sound like she came from anywhere, not the county, not even the South, but, not, *not* from there. She had the slow cadence that everyone else there had, but none of the twang.

"Yeah, no shit," Del grumbled. "How long have I been here?"

"Two days."

"Two days? How the fuck have I been here for two days?" Del shifted around and tried to sit up again.

The woman shook her head and walked to the bed. She gently pushed Del back down and expertly propped her up in the bed. "You've been here for two days because I drugged you, so you would lay still and heal. I can see that I should have kept you knocked out longer."

"That nasty goat piss you made me drink."

The woman nodded. "You're quick."

"Go fuck yourself," Del countered.

"Charming, just like your family."

Del's eyes flashed and she sat up. "I'm nothing like them. Just give me my shit and I'll be going home."

The woman smiled and nodded. "No, I know you aren't like them. Not totally, anyway. But you can't go home yet. You can't walk five steps on your own, and even if you could, Galen isn't done with you."

"Yeah, I know. And you're what, nursing me back to health so he can kill me later? I don't get why they didn't just kill me."

"That was their initiation. And, do you really not know they can't?" The woman looked at Del quizzically.

"Can't what? Kill me?"

"Yes."

Del felt the pull of her busted ribs and her head and arm throbbed. The light in the room was beginning to make her squint and want to cry. "I reckon they could. I think they almost did."

The woman shook her head, briefly left the room, then came back with a glass of water. She handed it to Del. "You heal too fast to kill like that. Your kind takes a shotgun to the head, and even then, it's not certain."

"I think you're full of shit," Del said. She sipped the water carefully. It tasted delicious, but it hurt like hell to swallow.

"Think whatever you like. How many people do you know that can have their ribs and kidneys smashed, skull fractured, and be mostly sitting up two days later?"

"I-I don't know. Maybe it wasn't as bad as all that."

The woman laughed. "It was worse. They beat the hell out of you. In fact, I've never seen him beat anyone like that." She sat on the edge of the bed. "You would heal faster if you hadn't been taking all the wolfsbane."

"What do you know about it?"

"I know it makes it twice as hard for you to heal. And I know it's going to take me a week to get you mobile. You want to know anything else?"

"I can't stay here a week." Del tried to sit up again but couldn't. She didn't want to stay. Just knowing she was within a hundred yards of the compound made her angry and sick. The added insult of not being free to leave was unbearable. But she had made a bargain, and she didn't know where Jerry was or what had happened to him. Maybe they wouldn't do much to him if she played nice, but the situation wasn't certain. Nothing ever was when it came to Nolans, except you could be certain that you weren't going to like the outcome.

The woman left the room and returned with a mug. She settled Del in the bed and smoothed the covers over, tucking her in as if she was a little girl. The woman handed her the mug. It was a hot tea. Del sniffed it. It smelled slightly like the other stuff, but less repellent. She looked at the woman doubtfully and hesitated.

"It's a weaker version of the other stuff. It won't taste as bad, and it will calm you down and help you sleep," the woman said.

"I've already slept a lot," Del said, but she was in pain and tired and felt like sleeping more if she could ever get her brain to stop churning.

"You're stubborn like a little kid. Look, Delilah, just drink it. Stop fighting this and it will go easier for you."

"I'll never stop fighting him. Not ever. I'm not in this forever." Del sipped the tea and leaned back into the pillows. The liquid didn't taste great, but it didn't taste like goat piss either. The woman had sweetened it. "And don't call me Delilah."

The woman smiled at that, but her eyes were sad as she

regarded Del. "I hope you're right. I hope this is temporary for you. I really do." Her tone was sincere, but just below the surface Del could hear the doubt, the resignation that said she didn't really believe it.

Del finished the tea and handed the mug back. The stuff was fast acting. Her eyes felt heavy and the pain faded into a dull throb. "You got a name?"

"You just now thought to ask?" the woman laughed. "Nina. Shut up and sleep."

Del closed her eyes and nodded. "Nina. Thanks."

"You might not thank me later," Nina replied. She may have said something else, but Del barely heard the words as the tea worked its magic and she drifted off to a peaceful sleep.

CHAPTER 9

THE SECOND TIME Del woke up, she hadn't slept nearly so long, but she felt a million times better. She could sit up on her own. It still hurt, but it was duller, and she thought she could hear a low hum and feel a buzzing vibration as her body knitted itself back together. Even Nina was surprised at the rate and progress after just a few days.

"You're healing quickly. Weird for how far from the Moon Cycle you are."

"Maybe I'm a prodigy," Del said.

"Oh, yeah. For sure," Nina said, rolling her eyes as she left the room.

Once Del was able to sit up and hobble out to the living room, she saw what Nina was. Del's Gran had been a folk healer too, a Granny Woman, versed in herbs and medicinal plants, remedies, spells, and useful little tricks that made living in the place possible. Del was a believer in all of it. She had seen her gran heal people more expertly than any doctor in a hospital, counsel people more thoroughly than a lawyer, and manage the impossible with magic. While Nina wasn't old, she was a granny woman, too. Dried leaves and herbs hung from racks and shelves. She had old jars, Miracle Whip, pickles, baby food, a few Mason jars, but mostly jars that Del knew were scrounged from the garbage and washed carefully to be repurposed for tinctures, tonics, and balms. Her gran kept every jar she ever found. She would send Del and Jerry out to look for little jars in burn barrels and dump sites. It wasn't just the familiar herbs and equipment that made Del know so. Nina had a cool confidence and iron will that was apparent in every word she spoke, just like Del's gran. And more than just that, Del could feel the prickle of magic about the place, a feeling she had always found pleasant and frightening at the same time.

She was still in pain, but less so. Del breathed deeply and let the smell of the drying herbs calm her as they always had. "You always done this stuff?" Del asked as she sipped a strangely pleasant, tangy dink that Nina had blended up for her.

"Yeah, I guess," Nina said. She trimmed bundles of leaves and tied then into tight sticks. "My mama did it. Her mama too. I never thought I would, though."

"How come?" Del asked.

Nina shrugged. "I hated it. Reminded me so much of these stupid mountains."

"My Gran always said that stuff got in your bones and your blood, and once that happens, there's no getting away."

"I wish she wasn't right, but she is," Nina said as she finished up her work, a dark, faraway look in her eyes.

"I'm getting away," Del said. "Soon as I get his money. I'm gone."

"I said that too, once." Nina poured a cup of tea and curled up in her chair.

"You got out? Why did you come back?" Del asked.

"You think it was voluntary?

"I don't know. Don't look like you're a prisoner."

Nina got up and stalked back to the sink. "You should know better than to trust appearances, Delilah."

"Don't get so touchy," Del said. "I just met you."

"And yet you're already making me want to choke you," Nina said. "You really are a prodigy."

Before Del could reply, the trailer door burst open and a steaming lump of a person was tossed inside. Junior came in behind it and shut the door. He kicked the figure and laughed. Del jumped up and lunged for him, but she was still weak and had no balance. He pounded her in the head and sent her flying into a cabinet. Nina was there in an instant and helped Del up and back into a chair. Her eyes scanned Del's face quickly, nodded at only minor damage, then turned toward Junior.

"There's no need for any of this," Nina said.

"You don't tell me what needs what." He slapped her across the cheek. Del came at him again and he punched her in the nose. Her nose crunched, ruined all over again, and blood spewed. Nina gave her a towel and bent her head back. "Look, just stop trying to help, ok?"

Nina looked down at the moaning pile on her floor then at Junior. "What do you want?"

"I thought I'd bring Delilah a visitor. I wouldn't have bothered if I'd known she was gonna be so surly." He grinned and pulled the blanket away from the lump.

They had kept him in the sun for a long time. Jerry was beet red. His skin was peeling and irritated, and his mouth was ringed with big scabbed over fever blisters. Even his eyes had a red, burnt look. Del had never seen him so miserable. She started to get up, but she was dizzy, and her nose was still gushing. She trained her eyes on Junior's and gave him every ounce of hate she had in her.

Jerry looked around for Del and smiled sadly. "I'm sorry Del. I didn't mean—"

"Shut up, dummy," Del said gruffly, but with affection. "I know you didn't. Everything is going to be okay."

"Sure will!" Junior said, clapping his hands slowly. "Delilah is gonna get us our money." He looked at Nina. "When's she gonna be done cooking?"

"She almost was, but then you had to smack her around," Nina huffed.

"You got til Saturday. Then they both get busy." Junior grinned at Del. "I can't wait to see how you do."

"Shouldn't be too hard. You're a total fucking idiot, so if you can do it, I can." Del said around the bloody towel.

"Ha. Cute, Delilah. Keep it up." Junior grabbed Jerry and hauled him to his feet. "Let's go, fat fuck."

"Wait a second," Nina said. She rummaged around her shelves and found a small vial of salve. She handed it to Jerry. "This might help. I don't know."

He nodded and took it, then wrapped himself in the blanket. "I'll be alright Del."

"You fucking better be," Del said, looking straight at Junior.

Junior laughed and pushed Jerry out the door.

CHAPTER 10

"Time to go, Sunshine." One of the morons rapped on the side of the trailer and started to enter.

Nina stopped him with a palm up and pissed look. "No way. You know the rules. You don't just come in here," she said.

Del smirked at him. In the two weeks that she had been staying there, she had seen Nina lay down the law to everyone in the compound, even her, most definitely her, except for Galen and Junior. The morons hated it. They made comments and called her a cunt, but she ignored them. She never actually threatened them at all, but they seemed wary of her, and while they talked big, they kept a distance.

It had taken a full two weeks before Del was able to move and breathe without wanting to die. Her body regularly went through a lot of abuse, but the beating she took was without a doubt the most difficult thing she had dealt with. She knew that while she would have healed eventually, she wouldn't have healed in two weeks without Nina.

"Ok, well, here," Nina said. She handed Del an old paper grocery bag. "I made you up some stuff to help. Keep using it. And use it every day after your change. It'll speed things up for you. Also, there's a week's worth of those breakfast things I make for you. Drink one every day. That will keep you going at the rate you need to."

"Okay," Del said. She didn't want to admit it, but all the stuff Nina had been feeding her was delicious. She wanted to ask about how to make the shakes, or whatever they were, but she was hesitant to admit to Nina she liked them.

"When you run out, come back and I'll have more of it ready for you." Nina narrowed her eyes at her. "I mean it. I'll send one of these idiots to haul you back out here if you don't."

"That won't be necessary," Del said. "I can manage myself."

Nina laughed. "We both know you can't." She poked Del in the chest. "You change in three days. Come back after the last night. I want to check you out. You should be totally healed by then, but I'm warning you now, the turn is going to be rough for you in this state."

Del nodded. She knew precisely where she was in the cycle and what she was in for. Her back and arm still ached, and her face was an ugly yellow bruise. The thought of what was to come and the pain involved were never far from her thoughts.

"Another thing. Don't take anymore wolfsbane. Ever," Nina said.

"Why?" Del shook her head. "If I don't then I get out for sure. It keeps me from changing all the way."

"No, it doesn't," Nina replied. "It weakens you. You still change all the way. It's just poison."

"You're wrong. My gran said it kept me from being like them." Del nodded toward the house.

"I don't doubt she meant well, but she knew it didn't do that. The tonic doesn't change that. It just makes you so sick you don't have the ability to heal as well. All it does is make it more painful."

"Nah. She wouldn't do that to me." Del started to walk out of the trailer. Nina stopped her.

"Hey, she wanted to help you. That was the best she had. It's the best I have, too. You are what you are."

"I'm nothing like them." Del felt the rage start to build in her chest. She growled and took a step toward Nina. Nina stayed still, not afraid at all.

"This seems a lot like them," she said quietly.

Del stopped and her face softened, then she blushed, embarrassed.

Nina stepped closer and put a gentle hand on Del's shoulder. "The turn isn't what makes you like them. It's the rest."

"Yeah, well, I guess I gotta go." Del turned to go.

"Go. Think about it. Come back and see me."

Del nodded but avoided eye contact. "No promises. But, um, thanks." Before she had to hear an answer from Nina, Del took off down the rickety trailer steps and shoved Fat Eddie Warner out of her way as she climbed in the truck. She looked back at the trailer as they pulled out, and was surprised to see Nina still standing there, watching her leave.

CHAPTER 11

BEING out of commission for two weeks presented several problems for Del, and she wasn't sure where to start with sorting it all out. She looked at the boxes around her bedroom. Half packed, haphazardly marked and labeled, the boxes were stacked oddly, large on top of small, askew, and at odd angles. Nothing about it was organized or spoke of a real plan to move. It was like the boxes had always known she couldn't get her life together and go. Everyone else seemed to know. Her mom. Shelby. Everyone at work. Even Jerry. He hadn't said much, just little shitty things every so often, posed little questions here and there that were clearly passive-aggressive protests to make her reconsider her decision to go. He was in league with the boxes. They were a quiet defiance to her forward momentum.

She picked up her phone. It had died sometime during

the first day she had been gone. She didn't think to ask for a charger, and even if she had, she had seen no evidence to suggest that Nina had the tech to help. She didn't even have a TV. Listened to a few classical music CDs, had an old flip phone that looked like the kind that used the refillable cards they sold at the Walmart. Not that Del was much more advanced, her cell was pre-paid too, but it didn't look like it came from 2005. Del plugged the phone in to the charger and waited for it to power on.

Nina was a puzzle. She knew more than just Granny Medicine. She knew regular medicine, too, and she obviously knew her lore. Del thought she knew what Galen kept Nina around for. She had seen several thin, skaggy girls show up. Nina quietly took them into a back room and when they came out, they came out with small paper sacks and whispered instructions about teas. Del knew those girls were the ones Junior ran. They lived in run-down trailers and RV's all up and down the Hollow. In those trailers, you could get drugs and laid and probably gonorrhea. Jerry sometimes went to them, but fortunately Jerry was immune to STDs. He also rarely had the funds and those girls didn't do anything on credit.

But there was something else about Nina, a far-away sadness under the steely, factual demeanor. Neither had been chatty about their stories, but Nina seemed to know a lot about Del without asking a single question. As soon as Del was coherent and conscious for more than four hours a day, they had settled into a quiet, steady co-existence that mystified Del, who could barely live with Jerry without threatening to kill him at least three times a day. She didn't guess it was that strange. Nina had seen her in a bad state; it wasn't like there was much need for modesty after somebody helped you go to the bathroom for a couple of days. But there was something else too, an easy familiarity that happened without anyone even trying. Del chalked it up to Nina being used to Galen and his idiots. Nina wasn't intimidated easily. She had taken zero shit from Del when Del had been at her grumpiest, and she wasn't bothered in the least by goons. The only person she seemed cowed by had been Junior. Del knew there was a story there, just like there was a story about the funny accent, and the big scar on her face, but Nina hadn't offered and Del hadn't asked.

Del's phone chirped and beeped as it finally had enough juice to boot up. When she looked at it she had a maxed-out memory from texts and voicemails. She rolled her eyes. She knew exactly who left them. She had used Nina's phone to call her mom, so only a few from the first couple of days had been from her. She had also called Skippy, and after listening to him bitch about how unreliable she was, she had lost her temper and told him to fuck off. She'd have to go see her mom, and she had to go drop off her two uniform smocks and pick up her last paycheck at the store. Those were pain in the ass errands, but they could be dealt with. The one that wasn't as easily dealt with was the person responsible for most of the messages.

Time could be marked by how angry and threatening

Shelby's messages were. Del listened to five of them and heard all she needed to hear. She deleted the rest. She had been dealing with Shelby for three years. It had never been easy, but at least in the beginning it had its fun moments. When she decided to finally move to Pittsburgh and go to school, she knew the breakup would be difficult, but she hadn't realized the anger that would be involved. She had anticipated Shelby's violent reaction. Shelby flipped out when Del was polite to the girl at the DMV, any girl really, so she got angry at Del roughly fifty times a day. Her anger wasn't a surprise. Del was surprised by her own. She had known Shelby would be difficult, but she hadn't been prepared for how pissed she herself would be about the gargantuan effort it was to disentangle herself from Shelby's dysfunction and move on. It was enraging and exhausting.

Del had broken up with Shelby no less than five times in the last month because every fight had seemed worse than the last, but every time Del told her it was over, Shelby wormed her way back. It wasn't like it was a mystery as to how she did it, and Del was ashamed of herself at how easily swayed she was by Shelby's persistence and skill of persuasion. The last couple of times, though, Del could barely stand to look at Shelby after, her own image in the mirror even less, and she hadn't even stayed the night. Still, Shelby would have to be dealt with, and if Del was sure of one thing, it was that she wouldn't make it easy.

She grabbed her phone, her keys, and her uniforms and headed out the door. She really needed to take care of her mom and Skippy today because Junior had summoned her back the next day. They had kept Jerry as insurance, which was smart, as they figured Del was going to run. She had been fully prepared to do that a couple of weeks ago. What was different she couldn't have said, but now she knew she wasn't going anywhere until it was all done. What done meant, she didn't know.

On her way to the store, her phone rang, and it wasn't Shelby or her mom. She frowned. "Hello... yes... no... no ma'am, I didn't get your message." She had hit mass delete on her voicemail without checking each one. That had been a big mistake. "Wait... wait... ok, well, I get it. Yeah...no, you can just send it back, can't you?" The lady on the other end got huffy. "Look, lady, it's my fucking money... no, fuck you. I'll cuss if I feel like it. You better send it back. All of it. No, you ain't gonna hold a hundred. All of it or I come get it and you won't fucking enjoy that." Del hung up and tossed the phone across the truck seat. It smashed into the passenger side door and clattered between the door and the seat. She punched her door frame as she thought about the old bitty. She'd lost the apartment because she didn't pay the first month's rent, being laid up as she was. In the back of her mind, she'd always known that was coming, she just wasn't quite prepared for the full sting of it. It set the tone for the rest of the day. She sat in the parking lot at the IGA and clenched her fists repeatedly as she tried to control her anger. It wouldn't be good to go see Skippy while she was this mad, but she didn't have a choice. She steeled herself and exhaled a few times before going inside.

Skippy was in rare form, a magnanimous façade over thinly veiled contempt. He droned on about his disappointment but was sure that things had worked out for the best. Del rolled her eyes and threw the shirts down on his cluttered desk. When he handed her the check, he explained in detail and with clear relish how he was forced to dock her for the uniforms and couldn't pay her for her three accrued vacation days.

"You gotta be fucking kidding me," Del said. "Look at my fucking face Skippy, does it look like I was lying about being in an accident?"

"Be that as it may, Delilah, rules are rules, and you did not work out your entire two-weeks' notice."

"You only scheduled me for four days anyway. What the fuck do you care?" She felt a slow build of rage in her belly, like a small flame, burning a hole in her stomach and heating up her entire body.

"I simply can't change the rules for you." He smiled at her, as if daring her to do something.

"Yeah," Del smiled and nodded. "Guess you can't."

She turned and walked out of his little office. She nodded at the ancient lady working in the deli. "So long Helen. Hey, you got a light I can borrow real quick?" The old girl coughed and produced a BIC lighter, yellowed with nicotine. Del winked at her. "Thanks, doll." She knocked politely on

Skippy's office door and went in without waiting. "Yeah, I just forgot one thing Skippy."

He looked surprised and his face was red. She could hear the porn he was watching on his computer. She grinned and looked around at the monitor. "Nice. Real professional." He had left the uniform shirts on his desk amongst the empty Mountain Dew cans, Doritos bags, and candy wrappers. Del picked up one of the shirts and flicked the lighter's wheel to produce a steady flame. Skippy just stared at her and she smiled brightly as the flame took hold. When the shirt was burning well, she dropped it on his desk and smiled as the papers and refuse caught fire too. The heat and smoke finally set off the sprinkler system and she heard yells coming from the store as the entire system kicked on, drenching the place in water. "Best of Luck, Mr. Bowman. Thank you for the opportunity," she said, smiling and happy as she walked out amid the chaos and panic.

CHAPTER 12

DEALING with her mom had been much easier than Del anticipated. After dealing with Skippy, she had been in such a good mood that nothing her mom said even fazed her. She cried and whined and claimed strokes and heart attacks. She also said she got a letter in the mail about having diabetes but Del didn't pay any attention. She looked around and decided this wasn't her problem to deal with.

"This place is a fucking pig sty, Mom. Get up and clean it."

"Delilah, you know I'm too sick," her mom sputtered.

"I know you're too lazy. Ain't nothing wrong with you. You can take care of yourself. I ain't doing it anymore."

Her mom's face got red, and she slammed her hand down on the old TV tray. "You won't talk to me like that! I'm your mother."

"You were a shitty mother. You didn't give a shit about me. I been taking care of myself my whole life, and now you expect me to take care of you. Do it yourself. I don't care no more." Del turned to leave and heard something whiz by her head. The old green ashtray shattered against the wall. Glass fragments and cigarette butts went everywhere, showering Del with stale grey ash. Del whirled. She growled and clenched her fists.

"I should have given you to him. I wanted to, but your gran liked to have a fit. I shoulda though. He woulda taught you some respect."

The urge to rip her mom's head off her body went through Del's mind. She imagined doing it, and just the thought made her feel unburdened in a way that she had never felt before. Then the image of her gran ran through her mind, then the image of Junior slapping Nina, and then finally Nina herself, telling Del she didn't have to be like them. She calmed.

"I spent enough time with him." Del snarled. "You can call him for shit, you think he's so great. Don't fucking call me ever again."

Her mom was still yelling and had made it all the way to the front door to scream at her from the porch as Del jumped in the truck and spun out of the drive.

CHAPTER 13

When Del pulled in her driveway, she immediately started cursing. Shelby's Camaro was parked in front of the trailer. The front door was wide open and many of Del's belongings were scattered on the small grey patch of threadbare grass. Del slammed the truck into park and stalked to the door.

The inside was trashed. Couch cushions and pillows ripped up. The kitchen was a mess, cereal and food scattered all over. Broken dishes, shards of cheap Walmart china littered the floor. The TV was smashed in. She could hear destruction going on in the back, and when she went back to her room, she found Shelby.

The boxes were all ripped up, their contents broken, strewn, and otherwise defiled. Shelby had a knife and was ripping up her pillows and scattering the feathers all over the room. She tore into the mattress, shoving the butcher knife down into the foam and ripping out big chunks.

"You fucking crazy bitch," Del yelled.

"Whore!" Shelby screamed. "Fuck you, you whore!"

"Shelby, I ain't gonna do this, so you really need to quit this shit and get the fuck out of my house now." Del tried to remain calm, but the hot ball of rage in her stomach was getting bigger and bigger as each stab ripped up more of her mattress.

"Fuck you, you cunt! You don't fucking tell me what to do!" Shelby screamed. She grabbed the small lamp from the bedside table and threw it at Del.

Del easily moved out of its way. "Shelby, I'm gonna call the Sheriff."

"Good, call him. He won't believe a lying whore who's been shacked up with some crazy witch out in the Hollow."

"He will when he sees the crazy bitch with the knife fucking up my house." Del pointed to the door. "Get out."

"I know you was out there, living with her. Fucking her. Lacy Janes seen you and she told Tammi."

"I don't care what dumb bitch told you what, you got no call to wreck my shit. And it ain't your fucking business anyway. I told you we're done."

"You don't tell me shit. I'll fucking say when we're done," Shelby screamed, then flew at Del.

Del put her hands up and felt a searing slash as the knife bit into her palm and forearm. Shelby brought the blade down in an arc and jammed it into Del's left shoulder but when she yanked it out and, then shoved it deep into Del's stomach, they both stopped and stared. Del stared down at the knife in her midsection, driven in all the way to the cheap wood handle and Shelby stood still, her face white and eyes wide as she realized what she had done.

"Baby, I'm... oh god... I am so sorry. I didn't mean to—"

Del really didn't feel any pain. As she looked at the knife, the only thing she felt was the white-hot rage that was emanating from the exact center of the stab wound. Its fire spread out in spider webs like a shattered windshield, and when it cracked enough, she screamed. Not a scream of pain, but one of rage that ended in a long, deep growl. She reached for Shelby and threw her at the door. Shelby crashed into the door jamb, bounced off it and into the hallway. As Del went for her again, Shelby scrambled around on her hands and knees and cried as she crawled down the hallway. Del grabbed her by the back of her shirt and part of her hair and dragged her the rest of the way through the trashed living room and out the front door. She tossed her into the side of the Camaro so hard her body made a deep dent in the door. Shelby screamed and slid down into the gravel.

Del reached down and pulled the knife out of her stomach. She stood there, growling, holding the knife as Shelby got to her feet. "Jesus, you... you're not—" Shelby stared.

"Go. Before I fucking kill you," Del said. She struggled not only to breathe, but to keep herself still, from ripping Shelby apart. Shelby had sense enough not to retort. She fumbled her way into the car and spun out of the drive.

Del was a mess. Blood covered her stomach where there was an ever-increasing red stain. Crimson bloomed on her shoulder and dripped down her forearm. As the rage subsided, she began to feel the pain and the effects of the blood loss. She felt a wobbly and far away. She needed help, but the hospital was forty-five minutes away, and multiple stab wounds tended to make them ask questions. There was only one place for her to go. She stumbled back into the trailer, grabbed some kitchen towels to stem the bleeding, then climbed into the truck and hoped she could make it to The Hollow before she passed out.

CHAPTER 14

WHEN DEL WOKE UP, she was back in Nina's crisp, white bed. Her shoulder was bandaged and so was her stomach. She heard the familiar classical music, sighed, relaxed, and then tested her ability to get out of bed. She was a little unsteady and dizzy, but not too bad, so she carefully made her way out into the living room, one hand on the wall as she walked gingerly down the hall.

Nina was sitting at her work table, picking through bundles of herbs. She didn't look up when Del eased down on the sofa across from her.

"You were barely gone 24 hours and somebody stabbed you twice. I don't think you're going to be particularly good at this job."

Del laughed genuinely. It pulled at her stomach and hurt. "Wasn't the job. I ain't even started the job yet. How bad?"

Nina shrugged. "They didn't know what they were doing or you would be in worse shape. You'll heal fine tomorrow night."

"Can I go home?"

"I'm inclined to say no. You're close to changing and we should keep an eye on the gut wound, even if you do heal. Also, you clearly need supervision."

Del rolled her eyes. "I'll be fine then." She started to get up. "Where's my pants?"

"Sit back down. You're not going anywhere." Nina finished with the herb bundles and went to the kitchen. She blended up a concoction and handed it to Del. "You put your truck in the ditch. Broke the axel."

"Well, then give me a ride." Del gulped down the smoothie.

"I'm not allowed to leave."

"What the hell do you mean, you're not allowed to leave?"

"I mean, they will prevent me from going to any other locations," Nina said. She sat back down at her work station and began grinding something with her ancient-looking mortar and pestle.

"That's nuts. Why?"

"Oh, because I will leave the first opportunity I get." Nina gritted her teeth and dug in harder with the pestle.

"Yeah. Who the fuck wouldn't? You mean you never leave this dump?" Del shrugged apologetically. "Oh, sorry, didn't mean—"

"Yes, you did. It's ok. It is a dump." She cleaned out the

ground herbs and put them in small baggies. "They take me to town if I have to go. Or they make me give them a list."

"You ain't always been here. I know you haven't."

"I grew up here. Over in Cambridge, actually. I left for a while when I was younger."

"What the fuck did you come back here for?" Del asked.

"It wasn't voluntary," Nina said.

Just then, Junior burst through the door. "Oh, good, looks like you're alive," he said to Del. "Get up. Got a job for you."

"She hasn't healed yet, Galen."

"She looks fine to me. Relaxing on your couch, sipping her tea." Junior grinned at Del and slapped Nina lightly across her face. "Get the fuck up and come on."

"I'm fine, Nina." Del finished her drink and rinsed the cup in the sink. Nina came back with her jeans and a clean t-shirt.

Del changed quickly. She felt a bit dizzy, but let her hatred of Junior steel her. At least she was starting the work. If there was a start, then there had to be an end.

"Only way out is through," she said to herself in the mirror.

She looked all right. A little pale maybe, but she was naturally pasty. She felt decent. The stuff Nina gave her always helped. When she came back out, Junior had Nina pressed up against the kitchen counter. He had his hand in the waistband of her jeans and was leaning in, pressing himself against her. She had her head turned, trying to avoid him, but not having much success.

"Yeah, so thanks. Again," Del said as she cleared her throat. The little spot of rage was back in her stomach and it made the stab wound feel like it was glowing with heat and hatred. She willed herself not to jump on Junior and rip him into as many pieces as possible. He laughed and slapped Nina on the ass.

"I'll be back when I'm done," he said. He looked at Del. "Alright Delilah, let's go see what kind of sand you got."

Del nodded at Nina, who whispered, "Be careful," and squeezed Del's forearm as she passed.

"Always am," Del said quietly.

"No, you're not." Nina went back to her workbench.

"No, I'm not," Del agreed as she followed Junior out the door.

CHAPTER 15

DEL CLIMBED in Junior's big black Dodge and wrinkled her nose at the smell of Skoal and Axe Body Spray. He fired up the diesel engine and Del cringed as deafening screaming and guitar blasted from the speakers. Galen Senior was all about low profile. Junior didn't follow the same game plan. Everyone knew his vehicle. It was the only one like it and it was always loud. You knew if you saw it parked outside a place to avoid that place because whatever was happening wasn't on the up and up. The cops knew it too, but they were so afraid of Galen, they gave Junior a wide berth, which made him look more competent at his business than he was. Junior drove fast, spinning and spitting mud and gravel everywhere as he tore down the road.

"Don't you want to know what you're doing?" Junior yelled over the death metal.

Del shook her head and continued to stare out the window. "No."

"Maybe that's smart of you and maybe that's dumb." When Del didn't respond, he just kept yelling. "Although I guess it doesn't matter. You'll do whatever, won't you?" He nodded at her. "Yeah, you will. And you'll fuck it up. I can't wait for that."

"I bet," Del said. She knew it was best to let him run his mouth, so she just kept staring at the road. Junior was easily doing eighty mph and they hadn't gone far when red and blue lights came on behind them. Junior laughed and cursed, but he slowed and pulled over.

"Stupid fucking cop," he said.

Del was inclined to agree. Nobody was dumb enough to pull him over. Well, almost nobody. Del shook her head when the deputy approached the driver's side window.

"You in a hurry, Junior?" Jacob Newsome was a friend. He and Del had been friends since third grade. He was big and burly, with red-brown, curly hair and a neatly trimmed beard. He had tried to get Del to sign up to be a deputy too, but she had laughed at the thought.

"Why no sir, officer, sir. Was I going too fast?" Junior asked.

Jacob shook his head and then looked in at Del.

"Del."

"Jake."

"You think I can talk at you a minute?" Jacob nodded his head for her to get out of the truck.

"No. We got someplace to be," Junior said.

"Oh, for fuck sake, don't get your old lady panties in a twist. I'll be right back," Del said as she opened the door. She walked to the back of the truck and crossed her arms.

"What are you doing, Del?" Jacob asked.

"Riding in a truck with an idiot," Del said.

"Come on." Jacob wasn't amused.

"Don't get involved Jake."

"Ain't gonna end well, Del." When she didn't answer except to shrug, he asked, "You know anything about setting the IGA on fire?"

"Don't even work there no more," Del said.

"Skippy seems determined you set the store on fire. We're supposed to bring you in." He looked back at Junior. "But…"

"I gotta go, Jake." Del turned to get back in the truck, but Jacob grabbed her arm and held her.

"Let me help, Del."

She pulled her arm free, shook her head, and smiled sadly. "No way out but through Jake. I'll be alright."

"I somehow doubt it," he said, but he didn't follow.

Del climbed in the truck, and Junior started it back up and took off.

"What'd your boyfriend want?"

"None of your fucking business," Del said.

"Wrong, Delilah. Until you are paid up, every fucking thing that you do is my business. And if it involves a fucking cop? It's especially my business," Junior said.

He pulled into a little rest stop with a single picnic table under a dilapidated shelter. The state had intended for them to be scenic little spots for picnics along the river, but the county did a poor job of maintenance, so they were usually just spots to buy drugs or get a blow job. There was a gray Chevy Cavalier— the most common, cheapest car in the area —idling at the stop. Mickey got out of the car and waved.

"What a fucking moron," Del said. Like they hadn't seen him and didn't know who he was. Whatever she was about to do, it was with an idiot, and even if it was rob a deaf and blind old lady, Del had a feeling it could easily go sideways with Mickey as a partner. She got out, but Junior stayed in. He motioned Mickey over.

"Go to Kitty's. Travis's got something for me. Should be two packages he brought back from up North. Some new stuff for us to look at and some cash." He looked at Del. "Bring it all back and don't fucking take all day."

With no more explanation than that, Junior gassed the truck and spun out, leaving Del and Mickey in a cloud of limestone dust. Del coughed and waved her hand in front of her face. She climbed into the Cavalier. It was disgusting. There were Taco Bell wrappers, pop cans, and junk mail all over it. The ash tray overflowed cigarette butts and there were clothes and more trash in the backseat. The whole car smelled like cheap drive-thru, menthol cigarettes, and body odor.

"Disgusting," Del said as she scooped the trash out of the passenger seat. She tossed it on the ground, figuring littering was about to be the least of her offenses. "You're a filthy pig, Mickey."

"It ain't my car." He lit a smoke.

Del grabbed it from him and tossed it. "No smoking in here. It stinks enough already."

"Look, just because Galen's your daddy don't mean you automatically get to boss me. I'm running this."

An empty Budweiser bottle was right there by her foot. All she had to do was pick it up and jam it in his eye socket. The hot rage emanating from the wound in her gut was demanding she do it. If he would have just said he was the boss, she would have ignored him, but bringing Galen into it had made it a whole different thing for her. That statement, fact though it might have been, blocked out everything else in her brain, and all it made her want to do was smash his face until he couldn't speak those words ever again.

But then she thought of Jerry. If she didn't get this thing done, she knew Jerry would pay more than her. And she thought about being free and done with the whole debt and being able to get out and start someplace else. If she sabotaged herself now, there was no hope. So she quieted the rage for the time being and resisted the urge to break the bottle off in his nostril.

"Well then run it, dumb fuck. Start with running the car. We ain't got all day."

CHAPTER 16

SHE KNEW where Kitty's was. Everyone knew where the only strip club for fifty miles was. Located off the main interstate, Kitty's sat back from the road against a hillside. Someday, after a hard rain, the big rocks in the hill were bound to come loose and smash through the club. Two gigantic rocks, one to the right and one to the left, had already fallen, but almost as if divinely protected, none had yet smashed into Kitty's.

Del didn't think it would take a rock. The place was cheaply made and run down. A stiff wind or spark would get rid of the whole place in a few minutes. The inside was dark wood paneling and concrete floors all lit by dim neon lighting. The stage was just a raised platform that made a U-shape all around the room. It reminded Del of a weird converted church basement. She supposed, for some people, it was a church of sorts.

The man that currently owned it, Travis Reeder, wasn't a townie. He claimed to be big city. He had a spray tan and he talked fast, so everyone just believed him. Del didn't frequent Kitty's, but she knew some of the girls from high school and they said that he was just from Huntington but lived in New Jersey for five years. He claimed to be connected that way and he acted like a big deal, but to Del, he couldn't be too big a deal if he worked under Junior.

She and Mickey walked in the club and she was surprised at the three patrons. It was 2 pm on a Tuesday. She really hadn't expected anyone to be there at all, but there was a toothless old man in a dirty straw cowboy hat, a fat trucker with a long greasy beard, and a skinny guy in a business suit. He had big wire framed glasses and a sparse comb-over. Del immediately thought he looked like a child molester. He was eating a sack lunch in a strip club, which was a whole pathos unto itself.

She nodded at her friend Charity—her actual name, no stripper name required—who came over and gave her a hug.

"What are you doin' in here Del? Ain't seen you in a minute." Charity adjusted her G-string.

"Looking for your boss. He around?" Del asked.

"Hey, I'm the one in charge and I'll say why we're here," Mickey said in a huff after he stopped looking at Charity's breasts.

"Well then stop looking at the pussy and say, you dipshit," Charity said. Del snickered.

"Where's Travis?" Mickey huffed.

"In the back where he always is," Charity answered.

"Alright, I'll go handle the business." He looked at Del. "You just stay out here."

"I don't think so," Del said. "I'm coming too. Sooner this gets done, the better."

"Well keep your mouth shut, then, and let me handle the business."

"Whatever, idiot." Del rolled her eyes and followed Mickey to the back office. He knocked, and when he heard Travis bellow, they walked in.

Pictures of porn stars lined the walls, some promo shots, some signed pictures of Travis and the girls. The place was surprisingly clean and well-lit compared to the rest of the bar. There was a lot of neon, but it looked newer and maintained. The office furniture was all black lacquer and silver. It looked like the cheap kind from a rent-to-own place that was meant to look fancy to people with no taste and a poor credit score. The desk chairs were black imitation leather with silver trim, and there was a matching faux-leather sofa against one wall. Del wasn't sure what was going to happen, but she knew that under no circumstances was she going to go near that sofa.

Travis was sitting at his desk, a large mirror in front of him, cutting out a huge line of white powder. He used a filthy cut-off red straw and snorted the line. He made a show of sniffing and shaking his head then addressed them. "What?"

"Hey Travis. Junior sent us," Mickey stuttered. He shifted nervously from foot to foot.

"So?" Travis went back to cutting out another line.

"Well, he said we was to pick up a couple of things you got for him," Mickey said.

"A couple of things I got for him? What? What couple of things?" Travis snorted another line; his eyes were wide and wild.

"Come on, Travis, you know, the stuff from Jersey."

"Mickey. Look, I told Junior I didn't have it."

Of course, he doesn't have it, Del thought to herself, *because it couldn't be as simple as pick up a couple of things.* "Well what do you have?" Del asked.

Travis snapped his head in her direction. He looked her over carefully; his eyes were wide and he had started to sweat huge beads of moisture. "You want a job sweetheart? Tryouts are at five. Otherwise, shut the fuck up."

"She's working with us now, Travis."

"I don't fucking care. I don't take orders from pussy. She can either get the fuck out of my office or suck my cock. That's her choices."

"No to both," Del said. The little place in her stomach wound was burning again. Junior sent her in here to this coked-out dipshit, knowing full well he didn't have the cash or the drugs.

"What?" Travis asked.

81

"I don't suck cock, and I ain't leavin' without whatever it is you owe." Del approached the desk. Mickey was shaking his head, all red-faced.

"Del, don't—"

"Shut the fuck up, idiot." Del leaned across the desk and pointed at the drugs. "You got money for all this, or this is the blow you were supposed to have for us?"

"Mickey, what'd you bring this cunt in here for? I got what I got, and what I ain't got, I ain't got." Travis reached in his desk drawer and Del's heart began to pound. She smelled the scents of metal and gun oil before she saw the pistol. Travis waved it around a little. "You think you can bring a bitch in here and order me around in my own place? Well, let me tell you what. Nobody fucking does that. You tell Junior I'm feeling very disrespected and annoyed right now, and I better not have to do anything about it."

The whole time he had been talking, the white hot little spot in Del's gut had been growing and growing. The pain in her shoulder was annoying, but the pain in her gut had been getting worse ever since he had begun rambling. She was sweaty and dizzy. She heard a buzzing noise and her stomach cramped. It was almost like she was about to change, but it couldn't be that. The cycle didn't start until the next day. She was at the side of his desk, listening to him run his mouth, a constant stream of insults and curses. Another cramp hit her stomach, right in the spot where her wound was, and she doubled over and slapped her hand, sweaty palm down, on the desk. Travis laughed, and she looked at him, but couldn't really understand what he was saying. It was as if he was saying it in a slow-motion nonsense voice, like the adults in a Charlie Brown cartoon. The only word she could understand was *cunt,* and each time he said it, her rage ball intensified. She dug her fingers into the wood of the desk. It creaked and popped and her fingers went through it easily, like they were digging through Jell-O. She heard *cunt* once more then grabbed the edge of the desk and flung the whole thing across the room. It landed against the wall and shattered all the frames and pictures. Papers and cocaine went everywhere. Travis dropped the gun as Del grabbed him by his neck and shoved him against the wall, squeezing his windpipe.

"Money and blow. Where are they?" He choked and flailed as he clawed at her hand, but she wasn't letting go. She squeezed a little more. "Tell me."

His eyes looked like they were going to pop out of their sockets, but he managed to nod. She relaxed her grip and he doubled over, coughing and wheezing. "Closet," he said.

Del nodded at Mickey. "Check it."

Mickey slowly opened the door as if he was afraid a killer clown might pop out at him. He pulled out a small, rolling suitcase and a paper shopping bag. The suitcase contained cash, Del had no idea how much, but it was full of smaller bills. The paper bag had three kilos of cocaine.

"That's all mine. Junior knows. He knows all about it. He's already had his taste." Travis held his throat and was barely able to whisper the words.

"He said to come back with both. He didn't fucking say they couldn't be yours," Del said.

"Fucking bitch," he whispered. Del shoved him so hard into the paneling that it splintered and cracked around his face. "Okay... okay..." he cried.

She let him go and he fell to the floor. Her stomach hurt again and she felt woozy. She motioned toward the cash and drugs and regarded Mickey. "Let's go, moron. You carry the shit."

Any pretense that Mickey was in charge was gone. He nodded at her, then collected the bags and headed out to the car. Del climbed in the passenger side and held her stomach. The rage ball was gone, and it had left her with torn stitches, five thousand in cash, and thirty grand in cocaine. Maybe she was a prodigy after all.

CHAPTER 17

"WHAT DO you mean you brought back cash and blow?" Junior asked. He looked at the cash and cocaine as if he had never seen either before in his life.

Galen was silent. He was cutting up a deer. His clothes were bloody, and his hands were red up to his elbow as he pulled out the innards. It wasn't deer season, but Galen wasn't worried. He killed whatever, whenever it struck his fancy.

"I mean, I brought back cash and blow, just like I was told. Way I see it, we're even now," Del said.

"Not hardly," Junior said. "That was always our money. You didn't make us nothing new."

He had been sore when she arrived back at the Hollow with the stuff. Del had another flash of rage when she pulled up and saw him coming out of Nina's trailer with his shirt off.

"What do you figure that coke is? That's new," Del said. "You don't even deal that shit."

"No, he was holding out. He owed us that, too," Junior said. "And we deal whatever we say we deal. That ain't no concern of yours. I tell you to sell a bag of dog shit, you fucking do it."

She saw how it was going to go. Every job was going to be something they were already owed, not anything new to earn back the debt. "You think you're slick, you piece of shit. But we'll see who's slickest," Del growled.

Junior glared and growled back, baring his teeth.

"Enough," Galen said. He hacked off the back quarter of the deer with a meat cleaver. "Take two off what she owes."

"Whatever you say, Daddy," Junior said. His teeth were clenched in a wide smile that his eyes didn't corroborate.

Del shook her head and flipped him off as she left. She slammed the door for good measure. Nina was leaning against the Chevy Cavalier, arms crossed.

She looked down at Del's stomach. There was a dark red spot where the stitches had torn. "I told you to be careful."

"I didn't get shot, so I'd say I was." Del didn't want to talk. The only thing she could see was Junior coming out of the trailer half-dressed. The little rage spot was blooming again in the pit of her stomach. She tried to get past Nina to the car door, but Nina didn't move.

"Come inside and let me look," Nina said. She put her hand on Del's as Del grabbed the door handle.

Del pulled her hand back like she'd been burned. "I'm fine. I just wanna go home."

"Ok, take it easy," Nina said. "It'll just take me a minute to fix it."

"Look, no, okay? I'm fucking fine. Thanks. You said yourself I'll heal up tomorrow night." She couldn't seem to look Nina in the eyes.

"Yeah, but that's a while, and I don't trust you not to get in more trouble."

"Oh, so you think I should stay here? No thanks. Wouldn't want to get in the way." Del shoved past Nina and yanked the door open. The handle popped off in her hand. "Fuck!" she screamed as she tossed the handle. She stalked to the other side, opened the passenger door, and then opened the other side.

"You're acting like an asshole," Nina said quietly.

Del laughed a small laugh. "Yeah, well, that seems normal for me."

Nina sighed, exasperated. "I don't think so, but whatever you say. Go be mad for a while. Change the bandage at least. Come back out here tomorrow for the turn."

"Thanks for your concern," Del spat as she started the car and waited for the wheezing engine to stabilize. "I can handle my shit. Been doing it all my life. I don't need a babysitter now."

"You need one now more than ever," Nina said, but

waved her away and backed up from the car. "See you tomorrow."

Del slammed the gas pedal harder than she intended and fishtailed in the drive. She yanked the wheel around and corrected, then gunned the engine and sped down the dirt road. She drove fast as she could. The rage spot grew and was joined by something worse. She pushed them both down, unable to deal with either, and let the noise of the wheels on the gravel road calm her. She thought for a minute, and instead of turning to go to the trailer, she went another direction. She grinned as the idea formed in her mind, pushing out the image of Nina and Junior together, and gave her hope that she still had a chance to get out.

CHAPTER 18

DEL FINISHED HER SECOND DRINK. It was early, and the only other people in the place were the bartender and two old queers who were always there. After her errand, she had been too depressed to sit at home in the ruined trailer. She knew that she needed to clean it up, but she had the itchy feeling she always got right before her turn, so she drove across the river to Owensboro, to the only gay bar within a hundred miles, a tiny little place called Cherry's Rainbow Connection, but everyone just called it Cherry's. It was lit by sad, rainbow neon lights and had strange blue carpet with an astronomy theme that looked like it belonged in a bowling alley, not a bar. Some of the bar seats were saddles, left over from a short stint as a country line dance bar. Del sat on a regular bar stool at the opposite end of the bar from the old queens. She signaled to Dennis the bartender for another drink. Dennis was busy getting money from Randy and Ellis, the old queens. Dennis was cute, she supposed, with a great body and nicely gelled hair that made him look fancy gay, like the guys on the Logo channel when they had cable for a month. At any rate, he was the best anyone in Cherry's was going to do, and thus, was royalty, which was why he was a shitty bartender unless you had a dick and money. Del had neither.

"Goddamn it, Denny," she yelled as she held up a five-dollar bill.

He rolled his eyes and huffed as he heaved himself off the bar in front of Randy and Ellis. He snatched her money then poured her another glass of Jack Daniels. "What are you even doing in here tonight, Del? Dyke night is Thursdays."

"Shut the fuck up, Denny. I can come in here whenever I want."

"Well I just thought you'd like it better if you was in here with your own kind," he said. He lit a cigarette and blew the smoke in her face.

She ignored it and took a big swig of her drink. "Don't be a bitch," she said. "Leave the bottle if you need to go sit on one of them old queer's cocks for your rent."

"You can't afford the bottle," he smirked. "Where's Shelby?"

"Far away from me if she knows what's good for her," Del muttered.

"Aww, you broke up? Again? That like the million and oneth time? Derek is back in town, huh?"

"Mind your own business, Denny." Del finished the drink and signaled for another.

"Everything is my business, sugar." Denny poured the drink and rifled through Del's money. He sighed and took all of it. "You girls. Hot and heavy one minute, tongues down throats and God knows where else, then boom, emo and mad as hell the next. I can't hardly even keep track."

"But somehow you fucking manage," Del said. She finished her drink and stood up. She was out of cash, and thinking about Shelby suddenly made her simultaneously sad and angry. She knew it was over, the stab wound had nothing to do with that, but she'd been with Shelby so long that a part of her was going to miss the consistency, even if the constant was crazy. She was angry with herself that even a part of her would miss it. She had met Shelby in this bar, and for so long, the two of them had been the only identity she had known. She'd made the conscious choice to leave, but there was this gravitational pull to stay. Familiarity and the idea of the known entity were the main forces at work.

"Don't be such a dramatic old lady, Delilah." Denny poured her another drink. "Sit your ass down."

"I ain't got no more money," Del said.

"I didn't ask for none." Denny nodded down the bar and winked at her. "I'll get those queers to pay."

Del gave a little laugh and sat back down. She had known Denny a long time. "Thanks."

He nodded at her and topped off the drink before sauntering back down the bar. She picked up a pen and one of the bar napkins. As she drank, she began to draw. Shelby's back, the dimples, the stupid tribal tattoo on her lower back, the butterfly on her right shoulder. She didn't draw the face. When she got to it, she left it undetailed, then the whiskey hit her a little and the anger in her stomach percolated a little more. She scratched out the face all together and left a big, angry blob of black ink where the face would be. She grabbed another napkin and drew a different girl. This one she didn't know as well, but when she got to the face, she found she knew it better than she had ever known Shelby's. She finished the drink and the drawing, stuffed it in her pocket, then nodded at Denny as she left.

She was opening the car door when something big hit her and knocked her into the side of the car. She caromed off the fender and slipped to the ground. Somebody kicked her. She screamed when a boot connected with her stomach wound. She snarled and grabbed it before it could connect again and shoved it backward. When she looked over, Derek was on the ground, cursing and sputtering as he struggled to get to his feet. "Fucking dyke," he yelled. "I'll kill you."

Both he and Del got to their feet at the same time, and he bellowed and charged at her again. She held her stomach and sidestepped him. He crashed into the side of the Cavalier and made a sizeable dent. He turned, swinging wildly at her, and connected with her eye out of blind luck. The white-hot place heated up again and she hit him back. He went flying and landed on his back ten feet away. She pounced on him and drew back a fist to hit him again, but someone jumped on her back.

"Leave him alone, freak," Shelby screamed as she pummeled Del's back and head.

Del dropped Derek and swatted Shelby away. When Shelby came at her again, Del backhanded her and she went flying into Derek.

"Next time, I'll kill you," Del said. She looked up and saw she had an audience. Dennis and the old men had heard the commotion and came out into the lot. "Stay away from me." She ignored the men and hobbled over to the car. She left them all staring at the taillights as she took off, head pounding, stomach aching, and eye swelling.

CHAPTER 19

D<small>EL WAS ANNOYED</small> when she pulled up at the Hollow. The late afternoon sun was still bright, and she hadn't started to cramp yet, but she knew it was coming. She could feel the strange tickle inside her, like things were moving and shifting. It was more pronounced than usual, and she didn't know if it was because she was healing or because she hadn't taken the tonic. She had none. Jerry was still on lockdown, so her supply was gone. Her plan was to hole up in the container and hope her need to heal weakened her enough to keep her from breaking out. It was a shitty plan, she had to admit. It was doubtful that she would remain locked up without the tonic, but she really didn't have any other choice.

Junior's call summoned her at 4 pm. She told him to fuck off at first, but he promised to set Jerry on fire and still send the goons to get her if she didn't comply, so she complied.

She slammed the door and leaned against the car, arms crossed defiantly. Junior was walking around shirtless, directing the goons here and there. The dogs were barking more than usual, and Del guessed it was the pheromones they could smell. She had never been around that many people about to change, and she was unprepared for the overwhelming smell in the air. She could almost see the waves wafting off all the guys as they ran around. As soon as she had gotten out of the car, they all whipped their heads around at her, so she knew they smelled her too. Junior walked over.

"I tell you to jump, you say 'How high'?"

"No, I say, 'Go fuck yourself'," Del said. "What do you want? I got shit to do."

"Nah, you don't. You're out here tonight." He grinned.

"The fuck I am." Del started to get back in the car. She didn't even get the engine started when one of the boys rammed into the Cavalier with a huge truck and a big, black grill guard. It destroyed the front end of the Cavalier. The hood buckled and crumpled like a tin can, and the engine smoked.

"You son of a bitch," Del yelled as she jumped out the car. "You can't fucking keep me here."

"Sure can," Junior said. "You ain't getting another ride."

"Why the hell do you care where I am tonight?"

"I don't, "Junior said. He nodded toward Galen's house. "He does."

Del stormed off toward the old house. She yanked the

rusty screen door off its hinges and kicked in the wooden front door. The whole place smelled like cigarettes, old man, and big dog. She always remembered the scent vividly; she'd smelled it before once when she had toured the county animal shelter during a brief stint in the Girl Scouts. The cages where they kept the big dogs had a distinct smell that she never smelled in the little dog area. That's what her dad's house smelled like: big dog, unwashed man, and Pal Mals. She paused a moment, and her skin crawled as she looked around. Animal skins littered the room and hung on every inch of the walls. She recognized cats, dogs, rabbits, squirrels, coyotes, rats, possums, coons, and deer. There were plenty of others she didn't recognize. She had always hated them. Galen skinned everything. He took pride in his skill at removing pelts intact. She knew there was another room, full of more than just animal skins. She'd stumbled upon it once, and when he caught her, he'd made her stay and watch him work. Sometimes the things were still alive when he did it.

She found Galen in the kitchen. He was half dressed, like Junior. Because she had barely seen him in the past fifteen years and mostly only saw him sitting, she forgot how big he was. Galen was at least 6'7", and he was broad, square, and heavily muscled for an older man. Junior was big, but not as big as their father, and while Del wasn't short, she wasn't gigantic like Galen. His entire torso was covered in big, ugly scars. Wounds of every sort were permanently etched on his skin, gunshots, gouges, slashes, and burns.

Galen wore them like some men wore tattoos. He seemed proud of them.

She had no idea how old he was. He shaved his head and his face remained the same, weathered and grizzled with an unkempt stubble, but always the same. He smoked a cigarette while he fried Spam. When the ash got too long, he flicked it off on to the floor. The whole place was disgusting. Trash, dirty dishes, clothes, and empty whiskey bottles were everywhere. He used to have a girl that came in every other day and cleaned, but he had apparently given her up because the house was a wreck. The trash was piled high on all the cheap furniture that he had ever since she could remember. It certainly didn't look like the house of the man who ran every criminal enterprise in three counties.

"Why the fuck do I gotta be out here?" Del yelled.

"Time you ran with your own kind," he said.

"I ain't nothing like you."

"We'll see. You stay." And that was all he said. He started making himself a crispy Spam sandwich with yellow mustard. He ignored her.

"Motherfucker," Del mumbled under her breath. She stomped out of the house. They had pulled all the vehicles across the road, blocking the drive. Del looked in a few of the trucks, but no keys. She swore again and looked up at the sun. She could try and walk out, but it would be too close. She looked back up the Hollow. The little trailers lined the four-wheeler trail that led back up into the mountain. She didn't want to do that either. It was here, where they would all be. She decided she was better off walking out. She could at least get somewhere else, away from them before she changed. She got to the end of the drive, but when she went to step out into the road, she stopped and got violently ill. She spit a few times to clear her mouth out, then tried to leave again. She vomited again, and this time, cramped so hard, she fell to her knees in the gravel. She heard a buzzing sound and her head throbbed and ached. She jumped when a hand touched her back.

"Back away from it. You can't cross it. It will just make you sicker." Nina helped her up and Del looked at her, confused.

"What?"

"I put it up. Keeps them off the road at least." Nina led her back to her trailer but stopped at the picnic table. She helped Del sit down and brought her some water.

"I gotta get out of here. I can't be around when it happens." Del sipped the cool water and felt a bit better.

"It will be ok. The only place you can go is back up into the woods. There's nobody past us for a long way." Nina rubbed her back.

"It won't be okay." Del looked at Nina's trailer. "I'll pop that thing open like a tin can."

"You won't. You won't get near me." Nina motioned in a circle. "I put the same around the trailers. "You can't hurt anybody tonight. Just relax."

"You'll be ok?"

"How do you think I live out here?"

Del sniffed and finished the water. She could feel the movement in her guts and the itch started. The next was the waves of cramps that were beginning to flicker through her guts. She felt beads of sweat start on her upper lip and forehead as the hot flashes hit her. She looked up at Nina and started to cry. She hadn't been this afraid since the first time it had happened to her when she was a little girl. "I don't want to hurt anybody," she said.

"You won't. I promise," Nina said. She took a few steps backward and waited.

The boys were all running around, starting to strip off more clothes, whooping and yelling joyfully. The sun dipped lower in the sky and barely peeked out from above the tree tops. Another cramp hit her, harder this time, and it yanked at her stomach, enflaming the stab wound. Del screamed and fell over. She felt hot, like her skin was burning, and she started to rip at her clothes. She clenched, and her body contorted and convulsed. She could feel everything moving and shifting and it was agony. She looked up at Nina, who was sitting on the porch step, calm and unworried. Her face was the last thing Del saw before everything started to rip and tear and become unbearable torment and pain. She let out a final, desperate scream and then mercifully lost consciousness.

CHAPTER 20

THE FLIES BUZZING and metallic smell in the air told Del everything she needed to know about the night. Well, everything she wanted to know, at any rate. When she opened her eyes, she saw that she was lying in a pile of guts. They were slippery, and when she tried to extricate herself from them, they seemed to want to come with her. She untangled her arms from the mess and stood.

What she noticed immediately was that while she was still sore, she was much less sore than she had ever been in the past. She slipped a little on the intestines and cussed, but when she stepped away from them, she stretched. It was pleasantly painful, like the first good stretch after a nice workout. Her vertebrae clicked in place, and she was shocked at how good she felt. She scanned the area and saw that she was in a little glade. Big pine trees ringed the space, and it was shady and cool.

The intestines, she was happy to discover, belonged to a huge deer. Parts of the animal were strewn about all over the clearing and the pine needles were soaked with blood in big patches. Del was covered head to toe in blood. It had mixed with dirt and pine needles which were stuck to her body in strange patches. All in all, she considered herself lucky. It was just a deer. Had she tried to walk home the night before, things might have gone differently. It could have been something else dismembered in the field. Or someone else. She sighed deeply in relief.

She felt her stomach. Nina had been right. It was healed over completely, only the scar remained. Her shoulder had healed, and her eye wasn't swollen or puffy at all. Her cast was gone, and she had full use of her arm.

She grinned when she figured out that she knew where she was. She could see the top of a tower a mile or so away. It was the old AM radio tower. They had climbed it as kids and had parties there with Mad Dog 20/20 and Boones Farm shoplifted from the Hasty Shopper in town. If she walked to the tower, she was only a few miles from the Hollow.

Walking through the woods in bare feet was less than pleasant and it was cold, but she didn't mind. She hadn't hurt anyone and she felt fantastic. Nothing really hurt that much, and she felt energized, a rush like she had never experienced any other time she changed. It was exciting, and she couldn't wait to get back to the Hollow to talk to Nina about it. She whistled and hummed as she walked. She made good time, and it wasn't even midmorning when she finally made it back. As she walked down the hill and by one of the trailers, a thin, rat-faced girl with a big cold sore handed her a blanket. Del smiled and thanked her, then wrapped herself in the blanket. She was grateful not to have to walk into the hub naked. Nina would have something she could wear, pajamas at the very least.

The boys were all back, lounging around a big fire they had built. They laughed and told stories as they ate piles and piles of food. Del was starving too. She wondered if Nina had any bacon. She could eat an entire side of bacon herself now. And eggs. All the eggs. Pancakes, waffles, grits, Honey Comb cereal, all of it. The boys cat-called, but the blanket assured her that they didn't get to see much. She flipped them off as she passed by and headed to Nina's. She paused to knock on the door, then stopped with her knuckled fist in the air when she heard the unmistakable sound of fucking coming from the open window.

She stood still, unable to move, and listened as he groaned and grunted and the trailer pitched and squeaked. Her face reddened and the little white-hot ball of rage in her belly came back. Images of the two people inside began to swirl in her head as the sounds got louder and more frantic. She was only able to move away when they finished. When he did, Del's fury erupted. She walked over to Junior's Dodge, grabbed the grill guard, and yanked. It popped easily off the front of the truck. She turned it on its end then rammed it violently into the radiator and hood. She left it embedded there, sticking half out, with coolant gushing everywhere.

The boys jumped up and started yelling at her. She grabbed Mickey by the throat and choked him until he gave her his truck keys. She wasn't sure she could cross the barrier and leave, but she knew if she stayed, she was going to be sick, so the net result would have been the same either way. She gunned the truck and had no problem passing the barrier. She drove fast and reckless down the road, not caring at all what happened to her or the vehicle. She cried all the way home. Tears of sadness and jealousy and rage streamed down her face.

When she finally pulled into the trailer drive, she was mostly done crying. She wiped her eyes on her blanket and sniffed her stuffed up nose as best she could. Her need was to be alone, but that wasn't to be. She killed the engine and stared at the familiar face leaning against the squad car parked in her drive. She exited the truck and wrapped the blanket around herself.

"Jake."

"Del, you gotta come on with me," Jacob said.

"What for?" Del asked.

"Shelby and Derek are dead."

Del closed her eyes and shook her head. "Fuck me," she said.

CHAPTER 21

THE POLICE STATION wasn't big enough to have one of the interrogation rooms like Del had seen on TV. There were three cops in the whole department, and only two of them were working. Clem Little was the ancient, fat chief of police. He was useless, but he knew everyone in the county, and the town council knew they were better off keeping the peace with Galen. If they hired a real cop, things were likely to get tense. Jacob was the other officer, and he was a go-getter, often causing trouble, much to Clem's annoyance.

There were four desks in a big room that had white cinderblock walls and bad fluorescent lighting. The harsh shadows made everything and everyone look more tired and haggard than they actually were. They made her sit, hand-cuffed, in an ancient office chair that was filthy plaid that had possibly been red at one point in its life, but Del couldn't tell. Del thought it smelled like burnt coffee and ass.

Jake let her put some clothes on, and she washed her face off in the kitchen sink, but she was still crusty with blood. They wouldn't let her shower and they took the blanket. Only the fact that Clem was an incompetent police officer was saving her at this point. Clem called in the state police—he had no choice—and the detective in charge started laughing and salivating as soon as he saw her come in covered in blood.

He was a real twat, with a cheap short-sleeved shirt that was too neatly pressed and a flat top haircut, all of which matched his condescending attitude. He kept trying to explain to Del what a world of shit she was in, outlining the two dead bodies, the witnesses at Cherry's that saw the fight, and the fact that Del was covered in crusted blood. He asked why she was covered in blood and where she had been all night. Del had never been arrested before, and as the Cop Twat pointed out, she wasn't under arrest now, but she knew enough to know that her best bet was to keep her mouth shut and not answer any questions. She sat and stared at him.

"Man, I never saw anything like what's been done to those two," he said. He picked up a folder and pulled out a picture. It was Shelby and Derek's house, the living room. Del knew it well. It was covered in blood splatter. Shelby had insisted on a white leather sofa, and it was drenched in blood smears. Del couldn't tell whose body parts were whose as they were strewn about the picture. Derek's head had been almost torn off his body. It hung by a flap of skin. Shelby's head was gone. Her body had been completely torn apart, the torso only recognizable as a human torso because of the butterfly tattoo on a spot of unblemished skin. It made Del want to puke, but she held it in. She tried to remain still and not to convey any emotion at all, but as much as she was over Shelby, she still hadn't wanted this to happen to her. The other question in her mind was, had she done it? Had she somehow made it all the way over to Shelby and Derek's house last night? She didn't remember, and never in her life had she ever had any control once the change happened.

She didn't know how long they could hold her there and keep yammering at her, but she knew they had to let her go or lock her up. They didn't even have a real jail, just a small room that served as a drunk tank. They held people there until the county jail bus made its daily rounds. Her head started to pound, and as the Cop Twat kept talking, she realized that this was how they got you to snap and say something. She didn't know how to ask for a lawyer, and she knew she couldn't pay for one anyway, not a decent one, so she bit her lip and struggled to keep from punching Cop Twat in the throat. He was in her face. She grabbed the sides of the ancient plaid chair. Her fingers popped through the fabric and the wood cracked as she squeezed and willed herself not to move.

"Officer, that will be enough. If you have further questions for Ms. Monroe, you may ask them through me." A tall blonde woman in an expensive looking black suit handed him a business card and smiled. She had short hair and it was slicked back. She acted as if she knew her, but Del had never seen her before.

"Her lawyer? She ain't even asked for a lawyer," the detective said.

"Oh, so you haven't informed Ms. Munroe of her rights?" the woman smiled. "I see. Well, that is telling. You haven't arrested her. If you don't have enough evidence to do so, then we are leaving," she said, offering her hand to Del.

"She ain't going anywhere. She's had issues with the dead couple and she's covered in blood."

"And that's your evidence, officer?" The woman laughed. "You have nothing. Good day. Come along, Delilah."

"The blood?"

"Did you properly sample it? Where is the chain of custody? I'd like to see it. No?" She shook her head at him. "Pathetically inept, Officer. Please charge her. I'd love to discuss your failure to follow procedure with the judge." He said nothing, and she grinned at him, a huge shark-like smile, all teeth, hunger, and malice. "Good luck with your investigation. Please don't hesitate to call me if you need further information."

Del stood up and let herself be led out of the station. When they got outside, a black Escalade was waiting for them. The woman got into the back and so did Del.

"Ok, who are you?" Del asked.

"Elizabeth Barton-Carr. I'm your father's attorney." She held out her hand.

Del shook it. "Where'd he find you?"

"Unimportant, Delilah. Let's talk about your situation. Did you say anything to them?'

"Nope."

"Did you allow them to take any samples? Blood, hair, urine, anything?"

"Nope."

"Okay smart girl. You're lucky they're hicks." She looked Del up and down. "I mean, you are fucking covered in blood."

"It's not human, so—"

Elizabeth held up a hand. "I don't care whose blood it is. It was probable cause to hold you. The old fat cop fears your father, and the state idiot must be on his first assignment."

"So, what do I do now?" Del asked.

"The same thing you always do. I'll make this go away. It's what I do." She smiled that predatory smile.

"How are you gonna do that? I did threaten them. I mean, hell, I'm not even sure I didn't do it."

"That has absolutely nothing to do with it. And even if you did rip them apart, I will still make it go away. That's what Galen wants."

Del's face got red and she felt the anger and hate stir in her heart. "I don't care what that bastard wants. I don't need his fucking help."

"Clearly, Delilah, you do. You're not a stupid girl. He doesn't call me, and you're sitting in county lockup until these knuckle draggers figure out how to try a murder case. Galen wants this squashed. You're fortunate."

"Lady, you don't know shit about me. Fortunate ain't ever a word I would use."

"Well you should. And I know everything about you. Galen has us keep up. You're his future, Delilah. He isn't going to leave you to rot in a prison cell."

The Escalade pulled up in front of her trailer and Del got out. "Keep a low profile. This will be a non-issue soon. I'll be in touch." Elizabeth smiled and offered her hand. Del declined.

"Yeah, well, just do your fucking job, then, you're so good." Del slammed the door.

Elizabeth laughed and nodded. "You are your father's daughter."

"Liz, say that to me again, and your head will be the one they're looking for." Del smiled back, then headed up the steps and into the trailer.

The very first thing she noticed was the smell. It was distinctive and had not been there earlier. It was the smell of pig manure and rot. She sniffed two places on her couch where it came from and knew that the Ring Brothers had been there. She looked in the trash can and there was a rotten rotisserie chicken carcass and part of a dead cat.

"Motherfuckers," she said as she grabbed the trash bag

and took it outside. She just wanted to shower. She wasn't hungry anymore, but she knew she needed to eat because she had two more nights to go. She really wanted one of those shake things Nina made, but thinking about that caused the blackout rage to threaten a return, and she didn't need that. Her phone was blinking with messages. One from Jerry, they must have given him his phone back, and one from Junior, screaming at her and promising her slow death for destroying his truck. She rolled her eyes. What she knew now was that he didn't have the power to do shit to her. Galen was much more involved than she had realized, and while Junior was malicious and hateful, and he would absolutely hurt Jerry to get to her, he wasn't calling the shots.

She had no food in the house. Shelby had destroyed most everything, but she thought maybe she had a few beers in the fridge. They would take the edge off her nerves and hunger. But when she opened the refrigerator, beer was not what she found. It was totally empty except for Shelby's head, sitting in the middle of the rack, blank eyes staring at her.

Del jumped and backed away. Her heart thundered in her chest and she felt sick and tingly at the same time as the adrenaline coursed through her. She'd hated Shelby at the end, but she'd never wanted this. The head had been severed clean. It wasn't jagged and torn like her kills were. She thought back to the deer head from the morning, and remembered the ripped flesh, hanging in strips from the animal's neck. This was different. Clearly a cutting tool of some kind had been used. The edges were smooth and even.

She wondered how Elizabeth Barton-Carr would feel about the probable cause of a head in her refrigerator. Bad, she surmised, so she didn't feel any need to report it. She did, however, feel the need to find a certain pair of ghouls and find out why they had killed her ex-girlfriend and left her head in the refrigerator.

CHAPTER 22

THE RING FARM had once been the biggest pig farm in the county, but now it was just a few barns with sad, filthy animals. Billy and Bobby had a half a brain cell between them, and their father hadn't been much smarter. He had sold off most of the family land and decent stock. At one point, the Rings sold pork to high end markets and restaurants, but these days, Billy and Bobby didn't bathe enough to make sales calls to fine dining establishments.

The boys lived in a world all their own. They took care of a bunch of filthy, inbred hogs, and they ate dead things. Animals, humans, it didn't matter to them. They thrived on roadkill and medical waste. Jerry had been friends with them since the sixth grade, which was about as far as the two Rings went in school. Del hated them. Not only did they stink, but they were idiots with a mean streak. Bobby ran over animals on purpose and Billy liked animal porn. She knew those things were probably the least worrisome things about the two of them. One worrisome thing was what made them put a head in her fridge. Neither was smart enough to do that on their own, and she didn't think it would take much to find out the truth, so she grabbed a baseball bat and headed out to the farm.

Their filthy old truck was parked in the drive. Del was somewhat unprepared for the smell of the place, even outside. There was an overwhelming stench of pig shit and sour milk. She knew the boys got spoiled milk from the IGA for free and fed it to the pigs. Milk jugs in big plastic crates littered the yard around the barns. The pigs all screamed and snorted when she pulled up, crowding at the fence, hopeful for a meal. Del tried to breathe through her mouth but gave up because she was afraid she might taste the stench. She hefted the bat in one hand and a grocery bag in the other, then steeled herself for the house.

It was even worse than she had imagined. Garbage, porn, and carcasses littered the place. She gagged and put her hand over her mouth. Billy and Bobby were in their underwear playing an old video game on one TV while porn blasted on another.

"Del, what are you doin' here?" Bobby got up. Del threw the bag at him and he caught it, then she bashed the TV in with the baseball bat. The porn mercifully stopped, and sparks flew as she bashed it a few more times for good measure.

"What the hell, Del?" Billy said.

Bobby fumbled with the bag and pulled Shelby's head out.

"You two, tell me everything about that head right fucking now," Del said.

"We-we don't know nothing about it," Bobby said.

Del crossed the distance between them quickly, wound up, and cracked Bobby on the thigh with the bat. It made a solid smack, and Bobby screamed as he fell to the floor. He dropped the head and it rolled around a bit while he writhed in pain and held his leg. Del smashed a lamp and then hit Bobby in the ribs.

"Who killed her?" Del asked. "You two are too chicken-shit, so who was it?"

"Junior. He done it. We just helped, is all." Billy held up his hands. "Come on, Del, we didn't have no choice."

"Oh, you did. Same as Jerry did. Idiots." Del bashed in the other TV and then pointed the bat at Billy. "Junior calls you again, you call me. You understand?"

"He'll kill us Del. If we don't do what he says," Billy yelled.

Del stayed calm. She smiled as she swung the bat. When she was done, Bobby was a tangled mess, still alive, but his limbs were all smashed and broken. "So will I. And when I do it, it'll be slower than him and it will hurt a lot more. So, when he calls, you call me. Got it?"

"I got it," Billy sobbed. He went to his brother on the floor and patted him. "Jeez, Del, you about killed him."

"Yep. I sure did," she said. "He'll heal. Feed him that head.

You tell anybody I was here, or what happened to him, and I'll feed you both to those fucking pigs out there." It was satisfying to smash things up and beat the shit out of Bobby, but the smell of the place was getting to her, and it was time to head to the Hollow to change. She left the boys crying on their floor.

On the drive out, she thought about Junior and his badly played game of chess. Framing her for murder? What good was that going to do? She was missing something. It was right there, but just wouldn't bubble to the front of her brain. She knew she'd get it, she just hoped it wouldn't be too late to do anything about it.

CHAPTER 23

JUNIOR CAME after her when she pulled in. She was expecting it. She knew it was all posturing though when he didn't come with a gun. She would have just shot him, had their roles been reversed.

She was smaller but faster, and this time, he didn't have the boys to hold her. She danced around him and laughed as he tried to catch her and failed. "Fat fucking loser," she laughed. "Not so big a deal when you ain't got help, huh?"

"I'll kill you," he yelled. "I'll burn that fat bloodsucker." He charged her, and had she not been laughing at him, she might have avoided him, but his rage quickened him, and her cockiness slowed her just enough that he connected. He knocked her to the ground and then fell on her. He wrapped his hands around her neck and choked her. She clawed at his hands and gasped for air, but she couldn't make him stop.

She was almost unconscious when he released her. She saw him fly backward and hit a big oak tree. He slid down the trunk, dazed. Galen was standing over top of her, calmly eating a sandwich.

"Y'all quit. Now."

"Dad, she—" Junior said. He got to his feet and came at her again.

Galen pointed a finger at him and Junior stopped. "I said quit."

Junior knew better than to try him. "My truck."

"She'll pay." He finished the sandwich. "Give her back the bloodsucker tomorrow."

"Nah, I won't, I'm gonna—" Junior was spitting, he was so mad.

Galen just looked at him and didn't say anything. The hard stare withered Junior and he backed down. Del stood up and coughed. Galen gave her a stare too. "You too, girl." Del knew it wasn't a suggestion. She nodded.

Junior saw the exchange and let out a growl and stream of curses. He took off into the woods. Galen ignored him and went back into the house. The boys stood around watching. They grumbled and growled at her but backed away and returned to their own preparations for the night.

Nina stood in her doorway, watching the whole thing. She motioned Del over. Del only had one image in her mind, and had a tough time looking at Nina and imagining anything other than Junior on top of her. She came closer but kept her distance.

"I didn't put the barrier up yet. You can come inside."

Del shook her head. "I'm good."

"No, you're ridiculous. Come inside. Please."

Del was surprised at the please. It wasn't an order or a hard, sarcastic please. It was soft and genuine. She nodded and went inside.

"You shouldn't antagonize him, you know," Nina said. She pulled a concoction out the refrigerator, poured a glass, and handed it to Del.

Del's stomach growled at the familiar smell and she drank it greedily. "I ain't scared of him."

"You should be. Careful of him at any rate. He's cruel, and he'll find a way to pay you back." Nina sat across from Del at the small table and watched her drink. "Why did you smash his truck?"

Del stared and shrugged.

Nina nodded. "Del, you can't be that way."

"What way?"

"You know what way."

"Why?"

"Why? What?"

"Why do you let him?"

Nina sighed and ran her hand through her hair. It was loose, and she nervously pulled it back and then around her shoulder. "I don't have a choice."

"What do you mean? Sure, you do," Del said. "Do you love him?"

"I fucking hate him," Nina spat. It was the first time Del had really heard her curse.

"Then, why?"

"Del. Just let it be." Nina got up and started to gather herbs and things.

Del stood up and grabbed Nina's hands. She stopped her, then gently led her to the couch and pulled her down. "Tell me. Please." It was the same tone of please that Nina had employed earlier, and it worked equally as well.

"My mom and my daughter. They live just outside of Columbus. Nice place. But they're not safe. He'll kill them if I try to leave again."

"Hide from him. He isn't that smart," Del suggested.

Nina shook her head. "I tried that. When I was pregnant with the kid, I ran. I thought I had a beautiful place in Massachusetts. I had Sammy. Respectable job, little house. He found us." She pointed to the jagged scar that marred her face. "Did that to me, which is nothing, but he tortured her, drowned her and kept bringing her back. I couldn't stop him. They held me and made me watch. Sammy was five. She remembers the whole thing. I had to promise to come back and stay. If I do, he doesn't bother them."

"I'll kill him myself," Del said. "Don't worry. I'm as strong as he is now."

Nina shook her head. "Not Junior," she said quietly. "Galen."

The bottom dropped out of Del's stomach and she wanted to puke. That was a different story.

She exhaled and looked at Nina. "I gotta go. We'll talk later." She stood up to leave and Nina grabbed her arm and pulled her back.

"You're thinking that you know the game they're playing, and you think you're playing it too. You aren't. Please, be careful. Please."

It surprised Del when she did it, but when she thought about it later, she wasn't sure why it surprised her so much. It had been inevitable from the first day. She pulled Nina close and kissed her. Maybe what surprised her wasn't that it happened so much as how it did. It wasn't that she wanted to kiss Nina, it was that she needed to kiss Nina. The wanting kiss, she was familiar with. That had been Shelby and the few other women she had kissed. Them, she wanted. Nina, she needed, and that was a completely different thing. For her part, Nina didn't seem surprised at all and kissed Del back. When Del pulled away, her face was flushed, and she was embarrassed at what she'd done, but she got over it when she saw Nina's smile.

"Go. Be careful."

Del nodded and headed out the door. "I will," she said, and this time, she meant it.

CHAPTER 24

"Ok, so, what the fuck are you saying? He didn't pay you?" Del asked. She was exasperated. Galen put her in charge of the women he ran all over the county. She and Fat Eddie drove all over collecting and keeping the girls in business. It was exhausting work. They were all high drama.

"No, he don't ever pay," the girl said. She had stringy brown hair and a crooked nose. Del thought she looked like an old lady.

"Crystal, look. Get his fucking money first. You know how this works."

"I try Del, but he hurts me," Crystal whined. "You gonna fix it?"

"Yeah, look, I'll talk to him. But it ain't free. I'm taking an extra five. And if you don't have it next week, all of it, you're out. Got it?"

"I'll have it Del. I promise." Crystal hugged her.

The girls all loved her. She wasn't sure how she felt about that. On the one hand, running girls seemed horrible. Junior and Galen kept them beaten down and poor. On the other hand, there was money to be made if handled right. The first thing Del did was tell them that if anyone wanted to leave they could, no hard feelings. Some left, most stayed. If they stayed, she knocked their kick down to fifteen percent. She kept Junior off them and dealt with any nonsense otherwise. Business boomed. They were keeping more and making more and overall much more productive. Del kicked ten percent and skimmed the five. She was sure the goons who had dealt with them before had skimmed more, and Galen was happy the revenue was steady. The ten percent of productive was better than the fitful twenty percent of what they had generated before.

The girls were also a fantastic network of information. They saw everything, and Del helped those that kept her well informed. Junior had just seen them as pussy and cash. Del saw the bigger picture. She saw information and power, if you knew what to do with it. She ran the prostitution in three counties. She knew everything about every dirty government official and cop. That was likely to come in handy someday.

She was also doing well over at the strip club. After her little visit to Travis and another couple of beatings doled out to him, he was complaint, and she was seeing regular skim from there as well. She put Charity in charge and the club started making more money. Travis was a shitty manager, but he did have Newark connections and that was Galen's interest.

One day she went in and Charity motioned her over to the bar.

"Hey Del, Travis has company," she whispered.

"Yeah? What kind?" Del asked.

"Greaseball kind," Charity said. "Go on back, but be careful."

"Careful is my middle name," Del said. She told Mickey to wait out front. He was too dumb to help anyway. She knocked on the office door, but didn't wait to be invited in. Two fat Italian guys in cheap track suits had Travis pinned to his desk, face flat on the wood with a gun to his head. "Yo, Travis-whoa," Del said.

"Who the fuck are you?" one of them asked. He pointed the gun at her.

"Take it easy, sir. I ain't here to cause problems. I'm here to help you solve 'em." Del held her hands up and smiled at them. "Del Monroe. Travis works for me." She loved saying that, and even with a gun to his head, Travis bristled at it.

"Oh really? Well, this piece of shit owes us ten g's. Plus, we had to come all the way out to Shitstain Hickville to get it. You got gs?" The big one looked her up and down and nodded. "We don't take trade."

"Hmm... yeah, I don't trade either. But I could help you

with your problem. And maybe make it worth your while to come out to Shitstain Hickville," Del said. She sat down in one of the desk chairs and relaxed, despite the gun.

"Oh yeah? How do you propose to do that?" He lowered his gun and relaxed too.

"Well, Travis here always brags about his friends in Jersey. I'm assuming he meant y'all." She motioned toward them. "Now I honestly don't mind if you kill this idiot, really, I do not care, and after we finish talking, pop him and be done with it if you still feel the need. I'll even clean up the mess for you."

"What kind of broad are you?" the big one laughed. He motioned to his partner. "What is this, Sal?"

"Beats me," Sal said. "Get to it, we ain't got all day."

"We'd like to expand our network. You distribute our Crank, we give you twenty percent. Maybe you got something you can unload back here? Alcohol? Guns? You keep us in the loop, we hook you up on the return trip."

"Fucking meth? That shit's for white trash shitkickers."

"And college kids and suburban moms. You got white trash up north, too. Nobody can afford blow all the time. Folks need value. I know you sell it. Where do you get it? Cartels?" When they didn't say anything, she continued. "That's a bad trip, way down south. We're closer and much less nervy than them Mexicans."

"You hear this broad?" Sal said. "Who are you to make big boy deals like this? We never heard of you."

"I speak for Galen Nolan. I know you heard of him," Del

said. "What if I bump it to twenty-five and the extra five, let's say, don't get all the way reported to your boss? Finder's fee, between friends."

"Oh, are we friends, Boss Lady?" Sal laughed.

"I think we are, Sal. What do you say? I'll even get you your cash today." She held up her hands and went to the closet. She knew the moron had money in there. She pulled out fifteen thousand and handed it to them. "A little extra, for your trip out here to Shitstain."

They took the money and shrugged, impressed but not wanting to show it. "Okay, let's be friends. We'll consider your offer and be in touch."

"Perfect. Enjoy your trip home, fellas. Drinks are on the house." She waved at them as they left. Travis cussed and sputtered.

"What the fuck was all that? You doing deals now? Junior's gonna flip."

"What'd you owe 'em for? Gambling?" Del asked.

"What the fuck do you care? That was money I owed Junior. What am I supposed to do now?"

"Travis, you are right, I really don't care why you owed them the money, but I'm glad that you did. It's maybe the one good thing you done for me." Del laughed.

"You stupid cunt. How do you figure that?"

"Well, if you hadn't been a degenerate and had paid what you owe, those grease balls never woulda come out here. Then I never woulda made the connection."

"You think those guys are gonna deal with you? They don't deal with women. Stupid bitch."

"I think they will. I was square dealin' with 'em. Everybody wins."

"Yeah, well what the fuck do I win? Now I just owe Junior more money, and I suppose you fucking want your cut? Well fuck off, Delilah. I think I'll just go tell Junior all about your dealing and your fucking skim."

"You're missing several important points here, fuckwad," Del said. "First, you think Galen's gonna be mad I just made that deal? He'd make that any day. Junior was supposed to close it months ago, which is why anyone has been tolerating your ass."

Travis paled under his orange skin. "So what?"

"And the second point is that now that I made the connection, I no longer need a dumb, spray tanned cunt like you." She grinned at him as she reached out and snapped his neck. The look of fear and realization remained on his face as his body fell to the floor.

She looked down at him, the unnatural orange of his spray tan, the piss stain in his crotch, and smelled the shit odor coming from him, and she felt nothing. He was a piece of shit. He lied, cheated, abused the girls, and did lots of other things that made him deserve his death, Del was sure. She just couldn't feel any way about it, about killing him. She wasn't happy. She wasn't remorseful at all. She just was. And that gave her a funny feeling in her stomach that she intentionally forced away. She didn't want to contemplate what that meant.

Del pulled out her phone and dialed. She waited for the answer. "Come out to Kitty's. Dinner's waiting for you in the office." She hung up the phone and went to find Charity. Somebody was about to get a promotion.

CHAPTER 25

DEL NEVER WANTED to touch anything in the Lion's Den. She knew how bad Jerry was at cleaning, and she knew how disgusting just about every patron was, so when she put her hand down on the counter top, she wasn't surprised to find it tacky. She lifted her hand and made a disgusted face.

"Goddammit Jerry." She looked at her palm and then at Jerry. "This place is fucking disgusting."

"It's a porn shop on the Interstate, Del. What do you expect?" He never looked up from the magazine he was reading. Jerry sat behind the counter with his feet perched on a stool, reading and sipping from a knock off Yeti tumbler. Del knew it was blood. Jerry licked his lips and bit the bottom one with each sip. He always did it when he drank blood. She didn't need to be able to smell the metallic scent to know what he was drinking. The act of it had always disgusted her.

He had healed just fine after Del got him back from Junior, and he seemed unfazed by his captivity. This was a particularly sore spot with Del as her entire life had been upended by him and he didn't seem at all sorry. He continued to work at the porno store and lump around the trailer. Del hoped maybe he was just overwhelmed with guilt and too stupid to see a path forward, but she was starting to have doubts that he cared enough to feel guilty.

A skinny kid with bleached blond hair and several facial piercings hovered around Jerry. The kid wore tight jeans and a tank top with a rainbow unicorn on it. He licked his lips as he watched Jerry drink. The kid would have been pasty anyway, but Del could tell from the dark red circles around his eyes that he had been recently turned.

"I expect to not get syphilis from a counter top, you disgusting pig," Del said. She shook her head at the twink. "Jerry, who the fuck is that?"

"Kyle," Jerry said.

"Does he fucking work here, or what?"

"Or what. He's mine."

"What do you mean, yours?" As soon as she asked the question, she knew the answer, and she knew she was going to be sorry that she asked.

"I made him," Jerry said. "He said he wanted it, so I gave it to him." He looked over at Kyle and glared. Kyle stopped fidgeting and sat quietly. Jerry waited a few seconds, then offered his Walmart Yeti cup to him. Kyle grabbed it and took a long drink.

"That's enough," Jerry yelled as he grabbed the cup from Kyle. Kyle slurped the blood that had trickled down his chin then cried out when he realized some of it dripped on his shirt and stained his unicorn.

"Jesus Christ," Del mumbled. "Okay, what the fuck, Jerry?"

"What do you care? You're leaving or doing whatever now. I just wanted somebody around."

"You're not gay," Del said. "And why is he acting like a fucking dog?"

"Oh, he's gay," Kyle said. "Real gay."

"Shut up, Kyle. You talk only when I say!" Jerry stumbled from his chair and tried to threaten Kyle with the rolled-up Hustler.

"Ok, enough of whatever weird fucking shit is going on here," Del said. She pointed at Kyle. "You, Twink, go on over there and look at cock rings, or whatever. Jerry and I need to talk."

Kyle put his hands on his hips and huffed. "Who the fuck are you to tell me what to do?"

Del sighed and cocked her head as she stared at him. After a few seconds, she started a low growl, then came around the counter and grabbed his neck. He squawked and slapped at her.

"Look, Kyle, just do what she says," Jerry said. "Jeez Del, he don't know."

Del let go of him and watched him scurry over and hide

behind a display of suction cup dildos. "Well now he knows," she said.

"I turned him, then told him that he has to do everything I say because I made him, and the only way he can die is if he doesn't." Jerry looked pleased with himself.

"That ain't even remotely true," Del said.

"He don't know that. He does whatever I want. Likes it. You should see what he'll do for a bag of blood."

"I do not want to fucking hear that." Del held up her hands. "Listen, you got bigger things to worry about than your boyfriend there. You owe fifteen grand and you're gonna pay."

He looked at her, his eyes wide and his mouth open. "But... Del."

"Naw, no buts. You think I'm just gonna earn it all back for you and you'll be clear to pound that twink all night? Nope. You're gonna work too, fuck stick."

"How am I supposed to earn that kind of money?" Jerry whined. "I can't just deal out of here. I tried it."

"You didn't try hard enough. You're gonna deal out of here." She handed him a Target bag full of little white packets, pills, and weed. "That needs sold by the end of the week."

"Del, I can't do that." He shook his head. "Buster will flip."

"You let me worry about that old pervert. I'll keep him in line. You sell that bag." She pointed back toward the nudie booths where freaks went to jack off. "Also, the price of them booths just went up. I want ten percent of that every week."

"Del, how am I supposed to do that?"

"Are you fucking stupid? Mark it up. Pocket the difference," she said. She watched Kyle slink around the DVD section and she got an idea. "I maybe got some other ideas too, but we'll start with that."

Jerry shook his head. "No. Nope. I ain't scared of you like everybody else. You can't boss me like tha—"

His words were cut off when Del grabbed his curly red hair and shoved his face through the glass countertop. She yanked it back up and against the jagged glass again. Jerry's face was a tangled mess of rips and tears that dripped blood everywhere. She held his head up and looked him squarely in the eyes.

"I love you Jerry, but you fucked up my life. You're gonna help me get it back." She didn't make any threats out loud, she just stared at him. He snotted out a bit of blood from his ruined nose and mouth and nodded at her. She let go of him and he backed away. "I'll be back Thursday night. Don't be short."

Jerry said nothing as his face healed. He understood.

CHAPTER 26

"YOUR FEET ARE COLD," Del said as she felt Nina snuggle in behind her. Nina's long arms wrapped around her and pulled her closer. She smiled and put her hands over Nina's, linking them together.

"They're not, you just run hot," Nina said. She kissed Del's shoulder. "It is cold outside though. Smells like snow."

The good thing about overseeing the girls meant that Del was able to work closely with Nina. Nina was as close to a doctor as most of the girls were going to get, or at least she was their first resource when dealing with problems. She could help most things, and when she couldn't, she referred them to an actual doctor. They all liked and trusted her, and Del liked watching her work. She had the same no-bullshit-matter-of-fact gentle caring that Del's Gran had, and she made Del feel calm and at peace.

It wasn't hard to see one another, but it was hard to do it alone and undetected. When the thing between them started, it was apparent to both that it wasn't going to be stopped, so they were careful and discreet. Once Del began working with the girls, she convinced Galen that taking Nina out to the girls made more sense than trucking all the girls to the Hollow and it was more low profile. It was also much easier to be alone. Currently, they were napping at Del's place.

"If we stay here, maybe we'll get snowed in," Del said. She rolled over, scooted closer, and buried her face in Nina's neck.

"You have four-wheel drive, and so do they," Nina replied.

Del didn't have an answer so she began kissing Nina's neck.

"No, don't start that. We have to get back. We've been gone all day."

"I don't care," Del said. She didn't stop.

"Yeah, well I do." Nina pushed her back gently. "Come on, let's go."

Del sighed and huffed, but she stopped and pulled back. "We gotta get out of here."

"Yeah, we do." Nina slid out of bed and began putting her clothes back on.

"No, I mean, like permanently," Del said.

"Impossible. I can't find my sweater," Nina said. She got on her hands and knees and looked around.

"It's in the bathroom, I think," Del said. She got up and pulled her pants on. "It's not impossible. I've got a plan."

"It won't work," Nina said. She pulled her sweater on over her head and handed Del her bra and shirt, which had also been in the bathroom.

"It will too," Del said, suddenly grumpy and offended that Nina was skeptical. "I've paid back the money. That's all I had to do. They got it all back and then some."

"Babe, I told you before, the game you're playing isn't the game they're playing."

"No, I know. Look, I figured all that from the start. I knew they would never square us up regular, so I've got other stuff going. They understand money. I've got enough to keep them happy and get us out of here. Sammy and your mom too."

"Delilah, Galen Nolan doesn't care about any money you generate for him. How do you not understand that?"

"Of course he does. Money is all he understands." Del finished tying her shoes.

"So, you think, what, you're going to go have a rational negotiation with him and barter for me?"

"Yeah. Well, I mean, no. Yes. I will."

"It won't happen," Nina said. "For someone so incredibly intelligent, you can be really stupid sometimes."

"What the fuck do you mean?"

"I mean, you are completely oblivious to what is going on. You can't buy your freedom, and you certainly can't buy mine."

"Then how do we get out?" Del yanked her coat on, angry at being scoffed at.

Nina wrapped her arms around her and pulled her close. She kissed Del and rested her forehead against hers. "We don't."

Del pulled back. "You're wrong. I'll figure it out." Nina said nothing, just shook her head, then laced their fingers together as Del led her out. Jerry was in the living room, playing video games.

"Hey Nina."

"Hi Jerry." She pulled her hat and gloves on.

"You know, you could clean up the kitchen," Del said. She located her keys and started for the door. She went out to start the truck and came back inside.

"You staying out of trouble, Jerry?" Nina asked as they waited.

"Trying to," Jerry said.

"He better," Del said when she came back in. "Look, clean this place up. At least the kitchen. You wanna be a filthy fuck, go live with the Rings."

"I might. At least they don't bitch 24/7."

Del rolled her eyes. "Give me a fucking break."

The truck was barely warm when they left.

"He is trying, you know." Nina scooted closer to Del. The heater in the truck didn't work well.

"He never fucking tries. I wouldn't even be in this fucking mess if weren't for his dumb ass."

Nina shook her head and sighed in exasperation as they sped toward the Hollow. "You really don't get any of this, do you?"

"What do you mean?" Del asked.

"Nothing, Delilah. Nothing."

They spent the rest of the drive in awkward silence. When Del dropped Nina off, she got out of the truck without saying anything and went in the trailer. Del wanted to follow, but the look on Nina's face told her she needed space, so Del decided to let her be. She had rounds to make anyway.

CHAPTER 27

DEL SAT at a high-top table in the Marv's Tavern and ate her hamburger. She watched CNN on the flat screen TV above the bar. It was the only modern furnishing in the place. Inside the bar it still looked like it was 1970. Antique neon Stroh's Beer signs and Advertisements for Pabst Blue Ribbon lit the dark wood paneling and American flag wallpaper. The jukebox still had plenty of Conway Twitty and Tammy Wynette. The crowning glory of the place was a massive shuffleboard table along the back wall. The thing was ancient, maybe older than Galen, and had years of dark sawdust piled around it. Del had always loved that table. Her gran brought her in once a week for dinner as a special treat if she was good. She always got a hamburger and fried mushrooms, which was what she was eating now.

The proprietor of the bar, Marv Huffman, was also a

blast from 1970. To Del he had not aged a day since she was a kid. His hair was still silver and black, slicked up into a low pompadour. He wore thick polyester pants and short boots that zipped up the side. Marv came over and set a draft beer in front of her. "Leona would whip the dog shit out of me if she saw me serving you."

Del nodded and smiled. "She sure would." Her gran had worked for Burt for years, and she'd threatened him with beatings and castration if he ever gave Del anything to drink stronger than lemonade. "Anyone give you trouble this week?"

Marv shook his head. "They behaved. Thanks, kid. I know you took care of it."

Del nodded. "Wasn't no big deal." When she found out the douche in the backward baseball cap, Owen Marks, who wasn't even from there—he was from Shadyside, three counties down river—was charging Marv a protection fee, she had a talk with him. At first, she tried to reason with him, but then Owen had called her a stupid slit, and she beat him with her baseball bat until he wasn't recognizable as a human anymore. Junior had been furious. Owen was his friend. Galen had just shrugged, but Del didn't like the smug, slightly proud look on his face. She fed Owen to the Ring Boy's pigs herself and felt oddly satisfied by it.

"Well, thanks. You need anything, you let me know." Marv nodded at her respectfully and left her to eat.

The bar wasn't busy. There was one old guy who Del thought was actually a corpse propped up as a permanent bar decoration, but he was the only other person in there besides her, and would be until old fogies started getting off work and coming in for a drink before they straggled home to their old ladies. All three of them, the Corpse, Marv, and Del, looked shocked when the door opened, and the mid-day sun poured through.

Jake stepped through the door and removed his deputy hat, then dipped his head respectfully at Marv. "Mr. Huffman."

"Hiya Jake. Burger?"

"Thanks," Jake nodded in the affirmative. He sat down at the table with Del.

"You sure you wanna be seen with me?" Del said around a mouthful of her sandwich.

"I never been sure about that," Jake said. He stole one of her mushrooms and popped it in his mouth.

"You always was the smart one."

"What the hell are you doing Delilah?" he asked quietly.

"Eating lunch," she said.

"Keep on being a smart ass. See how it works out. That State Police guy was beside himself about your lawyer." He stole another mushroom.

Nothing had come of the incident with Derek and Shelby. Del's lawyer had been right about that. It just faded away into nothingness. Elizabeth Barton-Carr was too good at her job, and the cops were too scared of Galen.

"Fuck Jake, that's old news," Del said. She finished her

burger and wiped her hand on the napkin. "I didn't kill Shelby and Derek."

"I know you didn't. You couldn't do that."

Couldn't she? Del wondered. She knew she absolutely could have if she was turned, but lately, she thought maybe she could have done it anytime. She felt flat about it. Maybe a slight regret Shelby had gotten hurt, but she didn't grieve.

"I know what you're mixed up in, Del. Let me help you," Jake said. Marv brought out his hamburger and Jake started to eat. "You can just stop. All of it."

"I ain't mixed up in nothing," Del said. She stole one of Jake's French fries. "Best thing, Jake, is to keep clear. I'm fine. Everything's gonna be just fine."

"Until it ain't and somebody else is dead," he said.

Del shrugged. "People die every day."

"Well, not my friends. Not on my watch," Jake said quietly. He looked her over sadly. "We still friends?"

Del smiled at him. Then she got up and threw a twenty-dollar bill down on the table for both their lunches. She kissed Jake on the cheek and ruffled his curly brown hair. "We'll always be friends." She turned to walk away, and he grabbed her wrist and stopped her.

"I can help you Del."

She pulled her wrist away gently and smiled. "I don't need no help." She turned and walked out into the afternoon sunshine.

CHAPTER 28

"WHO DID THIS, LILA?" Del said. She crossed her arms and leaned on the doorframe as Nina looked carefully at the girl's face. Lila had been beaten. Her nose was squashed and her eyes were both black. With her shirt off, they could see that somebody had lashed her with something. She had great red welts all over her scrawny back and sides.

"I can't say, Del," Lila replied.

"You mean you won't say," Del said. "Look, Lila, you tell me who did it and I go get him. You don't tell me, and it's two weeks in a row you ain't been square."

Lila's lower lip quivered. It was a swollen mass of cold sores and had been busted. "He made me give the money to him."

"Who?" Del put a hand on the girl's shoulder. "Tell me."

"Fat Eddie," Lila said. She started to cry.

Del patted her shoulder gently. "Jesus, Lila. Why were you scared of that fat fuck?"

Nina looked at Del and huffed. "Delilah, he beat her."

"Not that bad," Del said. "Look, Lila, I don't care who comes in here and says to pay 'em. If it ain't me, you don't fucking pay them."

"Del, I'm sorry and I know, but he—"

"No, no more sorry. Don't be sorry. Be smarter." Del tipped the girl's swollen face up and forced her to look her in the eye. "Hey. I come back Monday and you ain't got it, you're out. You understand?"

"Del, I ain't got nowhere else to go. Please, my face is all fucked up. I can't earn like this," Lila pleaded.

"Gimme a break, Lila. None of these fuckers care about your face," Del said with a little laugh.

"Del, that's enough," Nina said. She pulled Lila's shirt back down to cover the welts and gave her a little jar of ointment. "That'll help the lashes. The rest just has to heal." The girl nodded and sobbed. Nina hugged her gently. "It will be okay, just relax. Nobody is going to hurt you." Nina looked over at Del.

"Monday, Lila. I will be back." Del looked at Nina but patted Lila's head like a dog. "I'll take care of Fat Eddie."

It was a quiet ride back to the Hollow. Nina sat on the far side of the truck and stared straight ahead.

Del couldn't take the silence. "You know her. She has an excuse half the time."

Nina said nothing.

"I can't let anyone get away with that shit. Every single one of them would have a sob story if I let them tell me."

Still Nina remained silent.

"You ain't got nothing to say?" Del looked over at her and felt a panicky feeling in her gut as she struggled not to cry. "I got no choice in this Nina."

"Bullshit," Nina said.

"Bullshit?" Del parroted back.

"You always have a choice, Delilah." Nina turned and looked at her. "You don't see how lately you've made every choice he wanted you to make?"

"I just do what I have to, Nina. I do what I have to do to make this work."

"You think that, but you don't see." Nina shook her head and sighed as she scooted closer to the door.

"See? See what?"

"You don't see how much you like it."

"You think I like collecting money from whores and dealing with Tweakers and fucking degenerates all day?" She pulled into the Hollow and slammed the truck in park. "You think I like feeling like I'm gonna get shot or stabbed every fifteen minutes? I hate this shit. I hate all the back deals and skim and this fucking sneaking around." She pointed between them. "I wanna go. I want us to go."

"You know I can't."

"I don't fucking believe that you can't. I think you won't." Del knew that was ridiculous. She knew that had Nina thought it would have been possible to leave she would have gone at the first opportunity. She knew that if Nina tried, Galen would kill the kid and make Nina watch. She knew it with absolute certainty, and yet she still wanted to hurt Nina because deep down, she knew Nina was right. She did like it. She was good at it. Maybe better at it than she had ever been at anything in her life. She thought that should frighten her more. It bothered her that it didn't.

Nina didn't reply. She looked at Del for a moment with a sad and tired expression, then turned and got out of the truck. She went in the trailer and closed the door.

"Fuck!" Del yelled as she slammed her hands on the steering wheel. She pounded it a few more times, then got of the truck and slammed the door. She started for the trailer, to apologize, but heard laughter and stopped.

The boys were all sitting around a fire. Mickey and Donnie were passing a bong back and forth and Fat Eddie was shoving hot dogs in his mouth. They were all pointing at her and laughing.

"Aww, your old lady mad at you, Del?" Donnie yelled.

Del walked over and grinned at them. "Women," she said as she held her hand out for the bong.

Donnie laughed and nodded as he handed it to her. Del nodded back, and her smile vanished as she slammed the bong into the side of Donnie's head. The glass cut his face and her hand, and Donnie screamed and held his eye. There was a piece of glass sticking in it.

Fat Eddie laughed around the hot dog in his mouth. Del grabbed a hunk of firewood from the ready pile and hit Fat

Eddie in the gut with it. The hot dog spewed from his mouth and he doubled over. She hit him in the back of the head with the log then dragged him over to the pit. They had used an old tractor wheel to contain the fire. She slammed his face against the metal, and he screamed as it seared his skin. She searched his pockets and pulled out a sad bundle of cash. He only had a few hundred dollars, but it was the money he had taken from Lila. Del grabbed him by his hair and held his head up. "Next time you steal from me will be the last time you do anything, you fat fuck." She let him go and shoved the money in her pocket. She looked toward the trailer and started there instinctively, but stopped herself. She didn't think Nina would let her in anyway and that made her start to cry. She got in the truck and cried hopeless, resigned tears the whole way home.

She was hyperventilating by the time she got to her place. She turned the truck around and sped back to the Hollow as fast as she could. She sobbed as she pounded on the door. When Nina opened it, Del stood still and waited.

"I'm sorry," Del said.

Nina nodded and held her arms open. Del flung herself into them and hugged Nina tightly as she sobbed.

CHAPTER 29

"HOLY SHIT, that's five grand above what you did last week." Del finished counting out the money and grinned at Charity. "Nice work, Char."

"Yeah, thanks Del. I just did what you said."

"Keep doing it." Del counted out five hundred dollars, handed it to her, then gave her another five. "Give that to the girls."

Ever since she got rid of Travis and put Charity in charge, Kitty's had tripled its take. The girls seemed to take a personal ownership of the place, and Del started putting a little money into it herself. They cleaned it and spiced things up. The place was packed every night and even during the afternoons. Del also got the girls hooked up with a mini pharmacy and other ways to keep the clientele rolling all night and spending cash. All that coupled with carefully watered-down discount alcohol, ensured Kitty's was now a cash cow. Charity was sharp and great at keeping the other girls in line. All Del had to do was collect the money.

"They'll appreciate it," Charity said. She put the money in her desk. "Hey, Del, you said to let you know if anything weird started going down."

"Yeah?"

"Well, Junior came by the other day. He was sniffin' around back here, making remarks about the new stuff and shit you've been fixing. I gave him a grand and had Susie blow him and he seemed ok, but you maybe wanna watch your back."

It didn't really surprise her. She got word from all her sources that he had been following her and sticking his nose in places she worked. She kept her people paid up and that kept them loyal, so she wasn't worried. If he had been that smart, she'd never been able to cut him out of the game the way that she had. And anyway, he was making more money than ever. Del was kicking up enormous numbers. Galen, had he had any emotion to show, would have been described as giddy.

"Thanks, Char." Del gave her a kiss on the cheek. "Keep him fed. I'll make sure he don't bother you more."

"That wasn't what I was meaning. He's a mean fucker. Always was. And he fucking hates you. You need to be careful."

"I hate him too, and I'm mean."

Charity laughed. "You? Nah. You never was. You always

used to help that retarded kid on the bus. You was never mean to anybody."

Del thought about snapping Travis' neck and letting the Ring boys eat him, and how easily that had happened. She thought about Shelby and how little she cared about finding her head in the fridge. She thought about the beatings she doled out on the regular these days, and how much money she was making from running girls and selling drugs, how the last three months of turns had been glorious, waking up feeling alive, humming with energy, and covered in blood. She thought of all the terrible things she did, and how while she knew they were bad, still she told herself it was temporary and a means to an end. But truthfully, she was enjoying it. She was good at it, and that it wasn't even the money she liked so much as the hustle. She loved the hustle.

"Well, anyways, thanks." She handed Charity another hundred and winked at her.

Charity handed it back. "You ain't gotta do that."

"Maybe not, but I want to. Keep it up." She hugged her, then exited through the bar. Each of the girls gave her a wink and hug as she went. Mickey was waiting, and he looked at her and shook his head.

"You're fucking drowning in pussy. How's that?" He finished his drink. "They make me pay double."

"Because you stink and your hair's fucking stupid," she said. She whacked him in the back of the head. "And you creep 'em out. Try talking to them like they're people."

"I do," he said. He started the truck. "I'm nice to 'em."

"You stare at their tits and drool. Fucking stop being a weirdo and they might be nicer to you."

"I pay them, what do they care?'

"Well I wouldn't be nice to you even if you paid me." She pulled out her cell and looked at her messages. One was from Junior, a group message about the preparations for the turn. One was from Nina asking Del to check in once she got back. Things had been weird between them, not bad exactly, but just not like they had been, and Del didn't exactly know how she was going to fix it.

Mickey laughed. "Yeah, you ain't exactly nice, that's for sure."

When they got back to the Hollow, the rest of the boys were getting things ready. Junior wasn't around so Del headed over to Nina's. Nina was at her worktable. Del gave her a quick kiss and then went to the refrigerator. "Hey."

"Hey."

"You got any—"

"In the yellow pitcher," Nina said, her voice flat.

"What did you wanna talk about?" Del poured a glass and then flopped down on the couch. She took a long drink. It tasted a little funny, not bad, just a little bitter and maybe stale. "Tastes weird."

Nina shrugged. "I made it yesterday," she said.

"Oh, well, maybe that's it. What's going on?"

"I just wanted to make sure you were ready for tonight," Nina said.

Del stopped and cocked her head. Nina didn't look quite

right. Nothing did. The room took on a faraway look and then she felt a bit dizzy. "I think that stuff is rotten or something." She leaned over and held her stomach like she was going to be sick. She got up and tried to make it to the bathroom, but she couldn't. She puked in the kitchen sink.

"Not rotten," a voice behind her said. "Thought you were slick, huh Delilah?"

Del turned and Junior was standing there. He had something in his hand, but Del didn't recognize it. She tried to say something smart back to him, but no words came out. Junior reached out with the black thing in his hand and touched her neck. She looked over at Nina, who was crying. That was the last thing she saw as the electricity from the industrial grade taser coursed through her and she dropped unconscious to the floor.

CHAPTER 30

WHEN DEL WOKE UP, she was lying on her back, her head pillowed on someone's lap. She opened her eyes and stared up at Nina. They were sitting on a rough concrete floor. The walls were solid concrete as well, and a single exposed light-bulb dangled from the low ceiling to light the room.

"Where the fuck are we?" Del tried to get up and stumbled. She fell back in Nina's lap.

"Just stay still," Nina said.

"Nah, fuck that. Where are we?" Del pulled away and sat up. It was a bunker of some kind. The walls were heavy and solid. Chips and big chunks were missing from them, but they were so thick, it looked like the chunks barely mattered. The door was metal, on huge, solid, reinforced hinges. Dents peppered the massive door, but it was intact. She stumbled over to it and yanked, but it wouldn't budge. She pulled harder, as hard as she could, and it didn't move. There were deep gouges in the concrete floor all around it, especially around the door jam. Del recognized them easily. They were claw marks.

She whirled, panicked, and looked at Nina. "How long was I out? What day is it?"

"A couple of hours," Nina said calmly. She sat Indian style, perfectly relaxed.

"It's the same day?" She felt her guts start to shift around, tiny movements that signaled more terrible things to come. She pounded on the door and cursed at someone to let them out. The sound was stilted and squashed in the bunker, absorbed by the thick walls.

"They can't hear you and they wouldn't open it if they could," Nina said. "Just calm down. Come back over here with me."

"Are you fucking crazy?" Del yelled. "We gotta get out of here. It's almost time."

Nina nodded. "Yeah. I know."

"You know? Why are you just sittin' there, then? You know what's coming. I can't stop it."

"Nope. You can't. So just calm down. Come here. Please."

Del was crying. Not sobbing, but tears streamed down her face. She sat down across from Nina, dejected, with her face in her hands as she cried. "We have to go." Her voice sounded small and scared, like it had when she was five and the turn was coming. She felt the little ball of heat start in her stomach and she began to sweat. "I can't do this."

Nina reached out and took her hands. "I told you, you were playing a dangerous game with them. They were never playing the same game you were."

"Why? I did what they wanted. I made them money."

"It was never about that for him. It was about you."

"Me?"

"He wanted you. And I'm afraid now, he's going to get you." Nina pulled her close and cupped her face. She wiped a few of the tears away and then kissed her.

"Fuck him. I'm not- I'm not going to do this." A cramp hit her, and she doubled over.

"It's going to be ok." Nina said.

"It's not," Del sobbed. She doubled over again and screamed. "It's not going to be okay. Not ever again."

Nina kissed the top of her head and held her. "It is. After it's done, just leave. Please. Just get in your Jeep and drive away."

"After it's done?" Del screamed as another cramp hit her, and the heat waves started. Sweat began to bead on her face. She backed away from Nina. She tried to talk, but all she could do was sob.

"This isn't your fault." Nina crossed the distance between them and hugged Del close. "You have been the best thing in my life in a long time." She kissed her, then held her as Del cried. "After it's over, there's things I left for you in my place that can help. I promise. It will all be okay." Nina sat back down against the wall and waited. "I love you."

The heat was unbearable and the pain the worst Del had

ever experienced. She screamed and fell to the floor. She wanted to tell Nina she loved her too, but she couldn't make the words come out as she convulsed. She flipped over on her hands and knees, and Nina's sad smile was the last thing she saw before she blacked out.

CHAPTER 31

WHEN SHE WOKE UP, all she could do was scream.

They didn't open the door that day or the next.

She screamed continuously and sobbed the remaining two days and nights. When they opened the door on the third morning, she was covered in gore and her voice was gone, ruined from the screaming. She couldn't have spoken if she'd wanted to.

She walked outside calmly. Galen waited. He ate a sandwich as he watched her emerge from the bunker. He said nothing and neither did Del as she walked past him and into Nina's trailer.

CHAPTER 32

DEL PACKED up the last of her boxes and loaded them into the Jeep. She had a new one, a shiny black one that wasn't the flashiest, but was the best vehicle she had ever had. It was nice, but low profile.

Jerry stood beside the Jeep. It was early evening; the peepers were just out, and the air was slightly chilly.

"Why are you moving out there?"

"Can't stay here forever," she said. She closed the back door.

"You could. Don't go out there. She wouldn't want you to," Jerry said.

"Don't ever fucking say another word about her to me," Del whispered. She barely said the words, but the hatred and pain in them was as clear as if she had screamed them in his face.

"You can just leave now. You got money. You got a truck. Just go," Jerry pleaded. "You go out there and you'll never get out."

"I was never gonna get out," Del said. She climbed in the Jeep and slammed the door. "I want those three bloodsuckers cooking tomorrow."

"They just turned, Del. You can't give 'em a day or two?"

"Don't make me repeat myself, Jerry." Del didn't wait for a response. She pulled out of the driveway in a cloud of dust. She tried not to think about the fact that she'd imagined this moment, leaving the trailer park, so many times. Every time she had imagined it before, she was leaving for a city, she never fully imagined what city specifically, it was always just The City in her mind. Could have been Columbus or Pittsburg or any other one. Now she was going in the opposite direction.

She spent one night in Nina's place. That was all she could handle. The smells, the herbs, the smell of Nina herself was everywhere. She spent that one night curled up in Nina's bed, tangled in the sheets, so familiar and comforting at one point, but now, torture. She lay there and cried the whole night. When she got up the next day, she shut it all down, flipped the switch and got back to business.

She picked the nicest little house in the compound and told the whore occupying it to get out. Del paid her well enough, and by that time, everyone knew what happened, so the combination of money, pity, and fear solidified the deal. As soon as Del walked out of the trailer that day, she had been laser focused on business. She was fair to the girls and she wasn't cruel to them, but any pretense of friendship was gone, and she was like that with everyone, even Jerry.

To the ones where there was never any pretense of friendship, she didn't even bother. When she didn't take over Nina's place, Fat Eddie decided to go in and help himself to some things. When Del saw him coming out of the trailer with a box of items, she calmly walked up to him and beat him with a tire iron. She broke both his arms and legs and bashed his head so badly that even when it healed after the next turn, it was concave in a few places and his face had a permanent droop and twitch from the brain trauma. Nobody went near the trailer after that.

Del unloaded her boxes at the little house and walked down the path to Galen's place. He and Junior sat at the table, eating bloody, barely cooked venison steaks. He had left a third one on the stove for her. She ignored it, pulled a Budweiser out of the refrigerator, and took a long drink. The place was cleaner. She had one of the girls start cleaning again. Galen never said a word about it.

"New labs will be operational tomorrow," Del said.

Galen nodded and kept eating.

"Those stupid bloodsuckers can't cook," Junior said. "They're likely to blow themselves to kingdom come."

Del shrugged. "Who fucking cares. I'll get more."

"You start blowing shit up and the law's gonna to get interested."

"We don't pay them to be interested," Del said. "It's

handled."

"Well, I still say the bloodsuckers can't cook. Those are just junkies you had that faggot turn."

"Yup. And that crank don't work for 'em when they're dead," Del said. "They'll follow directions and they heal really quick, they get burned."

"Guess you thought of everything, eh Delilah? Head of the Class these days." Junior finished his steak then threw his dishes in the sink. They crashed and broke.

Del said nothing. She finished her beer, threw the empty bottle in the trash can, then tossed a fat envelope to Galen. "Jersey will be here tomorrow. Load of booze for their crank. Gonna see about a load of guns next time."

"Fuck you. The guns is mine," Junior yelled. He looked at Galen. "She gets the whores and the drugs, and now the guns?" He shook his head and growled. "No fucking way, Dad."

"Well, you could stop fucking that fat skank over in Beallsville, haul your lazy ass down to the bar, and make the deal yourself," Del said.

"A deal I didn't even know about til right now."

"So, I went to all the trouble to arrange a secret gun deal and then told you about it over your fucking supper?" Del drank another beer. "Sal said you didn't call him. He called me."

"Bullshit, Delilah. You fucking went around. If you think I'm gonna put up with it—"

"Shut up," Galen said. He finished his meat and handed the plate to Del. She put it in the sink.

"They'll be there around three," Del said. She drained the second beer and walked out.

CHAPTER 33

"THANKS, DOLL." Sal kissed her on the cheek. "We appreciate the help. Jimmy says anything he can do for you, you just say."

"No problem at all Sal." Del handed him a bag of cash. "We look out for our friends around here."

"Good month for everybody." He gave her a squeeze and then nodded at Junior. "You comin' up to see the shipment?"

"Be up there next Tuesday," Junior said. He sat behind the desk and tried to act like Del wasn't running the show. He had a sour look on his face.

"Yeah, good. We'll make sure you have a good time." Sal saluted him. "Brought you kids a sample. I know you don't go for blow, but this is good stuff."

"I don't know, Sal. You know how that stuff goes around here," Del said. "We can't move it as easy."

"Well it's yours to see about." Sal held up his hands and smiled. "We'll see you kids next time."

Del walked them out. When she came back, Junior was looking at the brick of white powder. Del ignored him and put the cash they brought her in a bag.

"I guess those greaseball guineas love you, huh?"

Del shrugged. "If that's what it takes, sure."

"What do you figure to do with this?" Junior held up the coke.

"Hadn't thought about it. Cut it and get the girls to sell it, most likely."

"Yeah, well, what if I want it?" Junior slammed it down on the desk. "I know you hold out, Delilah. Dad does too."

"What about you? He know about how you let those Mexicans come across the line and through?" Del smiled at him as his face got red. "Nah, he don't know about that, huh? Well I do."

"He wouldn't believe you," Junior said.

"Of course he would," Del said. "Hey, asshole I don't give a shit about your Mexicans. Just leave me the fuck alone. I ain't bothering you."

"I'm taking this blow." He flipped open his pocket knife and cut a little slit in the plastic, then cut out a long, wide line of powder. When he snorted it, he shook his head and his eyes went wide. Del smiled at him but didn't laugh when began to convulse and piss himself. When he was unconscious, she hefted him on her shoulder and carried him out. She threw him in the back of The Ring Boys' truck.

"You know where to take him. I'll be there shortly." Bobby Ring nodded, and the boys took off. Del went back inside and gathered up her money, careful to avoid the coke, cut with refined Wolfsbane.

CHAPTER 34

DEL LOADED the shells into the shotgun. If the smell in the bunker bothered her, nobody would have been able to tell. Her face was blank, an unreadable mask as she calmly loaded the gun. Nobody had cleaned up the bunker. It was still caked with gore months later, and it smelled cloyingly sweet and rotten.

Junior moaned and struggled. The metal rings that held him to the wall were heavy iron. Had he been full strength, he might still not have been able to pull free, not unless it was during the turn. As it were, he had snorted Wolfsbane. It didn't kill him, only weakened him to the point that Del had been able to keep him locked up. He was still sick from it, and he had vomited all over himself.

He opened his eyes and blinked. She smiled at him as the smell hit him and he realized where he was.

"What the fuck, Delilah?"

Del said nothing. She just stared at him.

"What is this? This payback for your whore? She was a whore, you know. Her whole life. Daddy spotted her early. He broke her in. I just maintained her."

Del remained calm. That seemed to make him more talky, which she thought strange.

"I never minded her face. Dad did. Only fucked her after a turn once we cut her up. I'd fuck her whenever. He only liked it after he killed somebody."

Del stood up and chambered a round in the shotgun.

"You gonna shoot me? You're a fucking coward. Afraid to fight me cause you're weak. Fucking weak-ass cunt. I'll kill you when I get out of he—"

Del shoved the shotgun barrel into his mouth. She smiled as she shoved it as far in as she could, until he was choking on it, like one of the girls in his porn. He gagged and protested around it, but he couldn't move. She was too strong.

She pulled the trigger and the back of his head exploded. Bits of brain and bone and burned flesh went everywhere. She was covered in gore and still she kept smiling. She smiled the whole time as she emptied shell after shell into the twisted, scorched meat of his head. When there was nothing left but a steaming stump on his shoulders, she dropped the shotgun. She went home and left him to rot.

CHAPTER 35

"GALEN, WE AIN'T SEEN HIM." Donnie shifted from foot to foot nervously. He almost never had occasion to speak directly to Galen. Anything he had to report went to Junior, and Donnie was spared ever having to converse with the big man. All the idiots felt that way, Del knew. They sweated at the thought of Galen even looking in their direction, let alone having to tell him that his son had been missing for four days.

"When was the last time you did see him?" Del asked. Even though it was only ten thirty in the morning, she had a beer and drained it quickly.

"We seen him Monday night." Donnie looked at Del, grateful she was the one doing the talking and not Galen. Galen said nothing. He ran a sharp, curved blade over the backside of a freshly skinned raccoon. It was a giant, fat raccoon and he scraped huge globs of flesh and fat off the underside of the fur. He flicked the lumps off into a rusty old coffee can and smoked his ever-present cigarette.

"He'll turn up," Del said. "Go make some rounds. I'll get with you later."

Donnie couldn't get out of the house fast enough. He bolted for the door and tripped over himself doing it, knocking over an old lamp.

"I'll check into some other places tomorrow." Del finished her beer and went for the door. "Gonna go check on the bloodsuckers."

"He ain't coming back, Delilah."

"Them Mexicans he was dealing with?" Del asked.

"Something like that." He said nothing else. He finished the raccoon and picked up another freshly skinned animal. He scraped it clean as he smoked.

Del didn't feel the need to say anything else. She left him to it and got ready for some business of her own.

CHAPTER 36

HE WASN'T STARTLED when he woke. His eyes opened slowly, and he smiled up at her, a weird, happy, genuine smile. Maybe the first one he had ever smiled, Del thought. She hoped so. She hoped it would be his last one too.

He said nothing and neither did she. She just jammed the thick hypodermic needle into his chest and slammed the plunger down. She didn't bother to pull it out, just backed away from the bed and waited.

Galen was still grinning. He sat up slowly and pulled the syringe out of his chest. The bed groaned and released when he climbed out of it, and his footsteps were heavy on the old wooden floor planks. Del expected him to drop over. She had loaded the syringe with a highly concentrated dose of Wolfsbane solution, or rather Jerry had. Just handling the syringe made her lightheaded. Surely it would drop Galen quickly.

When it didn't, she began to sweat. He advanced methodically. She backed away and kept some distance between them, but when she got to the bedroom door, he lunged at her, quick as a cat, and grabbed her throat. He backed her against the wall and started to squeeze. Del clawed at his hand and swung at his face, but his long arm kept her from connecting. She couldn't breathe at all. She choked and spit as she struggled.

Galen was sweaty and his face was red. His smile faded, and his grip weakened a bit. When it did, Del sucked in a quick breath before he was able to refocus and tighten his grip again. It wasn't as strong as before. Just before Del thought that she was going to pass out, Galen coughed and let go. He slumped against her, and the weight of his big body slammed her against the wall. They both slid down together, Galen on top of her, crushing her with his bulk.

Del coughed and sputtered. Her hands flew to her abused neck and she swallowed desperately. It was painful and brought tears to her eyes. She was still having trouble getting any air, but she was getting enough. She shoved hard and rolled his body up off hers enough to crawl out from under him, then slumped against the wall as she calmed herself.

She took a few precious minutes to rest; she knew she didn't have long based on how long it took the slurry to take effect. He was breathing fitfully but he was alive, and she needed to make the most of what time she did have, so she struggled to feet. She grabbed his big thick ankles and pulled him down the hallway and outside.

CHAPTER 37

DEL SAT CALMLY on the tailgate of the pickup and drank directly from an old Jack Daniels bottle. The label was gone, peeled off long ago in an attempt at Appalachian recycling. Now the bottle was filled with a viscous looking brown liquid that smelled like apple pie but would eat the paint off a car fender. It was delicious, her gran's recipe, and it was something that Jerry could brew correctly. She took a healthy swig of it and let the cinnamon fire work its way down her gullet.

She watched Galen carefully. He twitched periodically and mumbled as the sun began to rise over the tree tops. It wasn't light yet, but held the promise of a turbulent day, with the horizon bathed in deep red. Del remembered the poem her Gran always said about it:

Red Sky at Night,

Sailors Delight
Red Sky at Morning,
Sailors take warning.

She smiled, both at the memory of her gran saying it and at what it foretold for this day.

"How long you figure he'll be out?" Jerry asked. He eyed the horizon warily. He switched his gaze to Galen, who even though chained to the huge old oak tree with log chain, still scared the shit out of him.

"Not much longer because I'm gonna wake him up." Del took another slug of the shine then set the bottle down. She picked up a long cattle prod and a bucket of water. Del threw the bucket of water on Galen and he mumbled a little louder and looked like he was trying to open his eyes. When she touched him with the cattle prod, he screamed and thrashed against the chains. They strained but held him fast. He woke up spitting and sputtering, his eyes wide as he looked around and tried to figure out what was going on. Del stood still and waited. He finally calmed, and his eyes found hers. He didn't look hurt or surprised.

"You probably should have just done it while I was out."

Del shook her head. "Naw. I wanted you awake for it."

"It's always better when they know what's coming." Galen nodded in agreement. "The Witch taught you?"

"Yup," Del said.

"Well, get on with whatever you're gonna do, Delilah."

Del nodded and picked up a can of kerosene. She doused him liberally with it, then piled up plenty of brush, some bales of straw, and dry leaves around him and poured it on them as well. She stepped back, picked up her bottle of moonshine, and took a long drink.

Galen began to laugh, low at first, a chuckle, but then the joke seemed to get funnier and funnier to him until he was in a full-on guffaw.

"Why's he laughing like that?" Jerry asked. He seemed completely unnerved by the laughter. Del was unmoved and she shrugged. She pulled a lighter out of her pocket and lit one of the bales of straw on fire. It caught easily. She fed the fire calmly as it crackled and grew. Once the rest of the brush caught, she stepped back and took her seat on the tailgate again.

"Jesus, Del, you're gonna just sit and watch?" Jerry choked and wheezed as the smoke got thick. The sun was coming up and the red sky mirrored the flames of the fire.

Del didn't answer him. She just smiled and drank as Galen laughed and burned. She watched the whole thing, showing no sign of emotion or disgust as his skin crackled and charred. She thought he smelled like a hog roast she had been to once as a kid, only funny, like the meat had gone off before it was roasted.

It took quite a while for him to die. It was mid-afternoon when the fire finally burned out. Del took an old spade and bashed his burnt corpse to dust. She thought it would make her feel something, but the empty place inside her didn't feel like it had been filled up at all with his pain. It only felt bigger.

She shook it off and got to work burning down every other building in the compound, first his house, then the little trailer. Nina's place she saved for last. She made a final walkthrough and picked up a pillow from the bed. She smelled it and cried a little at the scent of herbs and Nina's shampoo that lingered there. She placed it carefully in her Jeep, the only thing she saved from the entire place. She didn't stick around to watch as the trailer caught fire and the entire compound burned.

CHAPTER 38

DEL PULLED up in front of the little white house in Grove-port. It wasn't fancy at all, small little place, not a particularly nice yard, and it could have used a coat of paint, but it was otherwise neat and tidy. A well-worn bicycle was on its side in the drive. Del picked it up on her way in and propped it up on its kick stand. The bike was a little boy's BMX, but it had pink handgrips and a purple seat.

She delayed making the trip as long as she could, but in the end, she knew this was the last piece of business she needed to take care of, and she needed it done. Three times on the drive she had almost turned around and gone back home, but her thoughts went to Nina, and she turned the car around and continued toward her final task.

She paused before the concrete steps that led up to the

porch. She had no idea what she was going to say and even less idea of what to expect them to say. She couldn't tell them what really happened. She could barely admit it to herself. She thought of how Nina had been at the end, in control, calm, loving, and suddenly Del was ashamed of herself for her cowardice. She closed her eyes, exhaled, and willed herself up the steps. When she got close to the door, she felt a familiar sickness and she swallowed down bile as she calmed herself. He hands shook as she opened the screen door and knocked lightly.

It seemed like it took forever; but finally, a tall gaunt woman opened the door. Nina had resembled her mother. They had the same body type, and Del thought they had once had the same color hair—the older woman's was ashy grey— but their faces were totally different. This woman's face was lumpy, like a potato, and her eyes were deep brown. Maybe if Nina had been standing beside her, Del would have been able to see more of a resemblance, but right then, she couldn't.

The woman knew exactly who Del was the minute she laid eyes on her, and Del watched as the older woman's face grew cold. Her eyes flashed with hatred. "You leave us alone."

"I didn't come to hurt nobody," Del said.

"Like I'd trust any Nolan that said that," the woman spat. "Go away."

"I am. I mean, I will, I wanted to tell you," she looked at the woman's face contorted with hate, and she fumbled for the words, "Nobody is going to come after you. Not ever again."

"Where's Nina?" the woman asked.

Del couldn't form the words to tell her. She just looked at her. The woman began sobbing as she understood, and Del just stood there. She couldn't help. She couldn't help herself let alone a mother who just realized her child was never coming home.

"I'm sorry," was all Del could croak out. They were the sincerest words she had ever spoken in her life.

The old lady didn't say anything, she just sobbed. Del heard a noise from the upstairs of the house. A small blonde head wormed its way into the door frame and around the old woman.

"Gram, what's wrong?" the little voice asked.

Del's mom had been terrible at keeping photos, but she had kept enough so that Del knew that if you put a picture of a seven-year-old Delilah Monroe up next to a picture of the little girl standing before her now, you would be hard pressed to tell the difference between the two. They were almost identical, with the same coloring, same build, same hair, even the same face all except one thing. Nina's hazel eyes stared back at her from the little girl's face. They were so strikingly Nina's eyes that Del could barely look at her, could barely form a thought, and could barely keep herself from screaming.

She wanted to tell the old woman not to worry, that she wouldn't ever have to worry about anything ever again, but she couldn't. She bit her lip, tamped down the screams and sobs deep inside her, and left the old woman and the little girl, her little sister, standing on that porch in Groveport. As she got in the Jeep and drove back home, she willed herself to feel nothing, and hoped that she wouldn't be able to feel anything ever again.

CHAPTER 39

THE NEW HOUSE was all the way on top of the hill. It was a custom log cabin, brought up the mountain piece by piece. The whole front of it was open windows and the view stunning as it looked out over the river valley and the tiny town below. Del liked to sleep there. Her bed was in the great room, so she could see out those big windows. She sat in front of them in a chair and watched the sun come up.

A form in the bed behind her stirred. She wouldn't sleep in the bed while somebody else was in it, and usually she just kicked them out when she was bored with them. Last night had been Charity, and she was never as brusque with her as she was with the others. Still, Charity knew the rules, and as soon as she woke up, didn't dally in getting dressed and getting gone. She paused and squeezed Del's shoulder. "Sorry Del. Fell asleep."

"It's fine. I'll send Davey down later to help you with that thing."

Charity nodded. "Thanks. I'll tell the girls hey for you."

"Whatever," Del said as she got up and pulled on her jeans. "Later."

Charity paused and looked like she was going to cry. "You know, you don't have to—" She stopped and bit her lip as Del stared at her. Del didn't make a move or threaten Charity in any way, she just stayed unbearably still and stared. Charity let out a little sob, but Del ignored her and turned back around to the window to watch the sun come up.

"Later," Charity said. She picked up her things and left. She passed Jerry in the hall and he nodded at her sadly.

He steeled himself and approached Del carefully. She didn't turn around and look at him, she just continued to stare out the window. She sipped her favorite morning drink, the shakes Nina would make. Nina had left her the recipe. Del could never figure out why they tasted so good or why she felt so amazing after she drank one. Nina had neglected to tell her the whole time it had been a blend of fruits and human flesh. She'd been sick at first when she read the note, but she tamped her emotion and disgust down and tucked them away. They were of no more use to her in life and the drink kept her strong.

"Everything went fine last night," he said.

"Good. You get those new guys set up?"

"Yes."

"The idiot who blew himself up?"

"He's fucked up, but he'll heal. Jake was asking him some questions."

"Burn him, then." Del said. "I'll handle the Sheriff."

"He won't say nothing Del."

"Why chance it? I want it done. Today. Where's he stay?"

"Over on Walnut with his mom."

"Get rid of them both."

"Jesus, Del."

"You do it or I will. Give them to the Rings when you're done. They'll keep it clean."

"Why?"

"I don't like messes." Del pulled on her shoes and picked up her keys. "I'll be at the office. Get it done before you go to bed."

"You don't gotta be this way, Del." He grabbed her arm as she passed him and held her. "This ain't you."

"Yeah, it is, and always was," Del said. She jerked her arm away from him and headed out into the cool, foggy spring morning. She had business elsewhere.

ACKNOWLEDGMENTS

I can say with 100% certainty that this book wouldn't have been possible without one particular person. Jae, this wouldn't have happened without you. You gave encouragement, advice, mad editing skills, and motivation. When we started Denny's-ing in January, I didn't imagine that I would write so much that I could publish two books in less than a year. It's been crazy productive and more fun than I thought possible. You make me want to be a better writer and a better person. Thanks just aren't enough, but you refuse to see reason and my math skills, so this will have to do.

ABOUT THE AUTHOR

Jessica Raney is an author of speculative fiction. She has two collections of short stories: *Oddballs: A Collection of Short Fiction* and *Dreadful Pennies: A Collection of Short Things*. Her work has also appeared in the anthology, *Hair Raising Tales of Horror*. When not navigating Houston traffic or writing, she's dealing with her cat/dog/demon/baby, Gimli.